Prayer for the Wild

by

Scott Martinez

www.trafford.com
North America & international
toll-free: 1 888 232 4444 (USA & Canada)
fax: 812 355 4082

. . . cause Love is all good people need
Music sets the sick ones free
without Love no one ever grows
nothing ever sings . . .

-Mother Love Bone-

1

Give it to me.

That sweet sound, the gentle groove, play me, my breath and body, take me home, past words, where everything's a glimpse and a traveling insight, where all good things end.

A burning hue filled the space, and the lifting fog left her drenched, spent, with nothing more to give, save one final note that resonated past the beat, rhythm, and words, passing the red and into pitch black. There was a splinter of silence, the slightest pause, then an eruption of roaring applause as the house lights brightened, illuminating the dingy smoke-stained club. She stepped back onto the slight proscenium to a clamor of laughs, screams and greetings.

Piper Wild was fearless, a person who needn't move to captivate, a performer whose every breath and gesture resonated on the edge of physical violence.

But this part of the band's ending bit, to leave her guitar sitting center in a pool of red light and a loud shock of feedback amongst the otherwise tossed stage, was way too much. A great effect, but the few moments it took for the lights to go black, the band to exit, the crowd to scream, and for her to get back onstage to it, seemed forever. It could get knocked over, or worse, she wanted only to save her guitar.

At a show like this beer bottles might shower a stage in appreciation, and that guitar, her hollow-body electric Gretch, its custom Cadillac green finish weathered into a cold forest black, was irreplaceable. Where was her head? What would she do if it was ruined?

No way was any dog-and-pony gig in a sweat-box like this worth risking her ax, not now, not again, not ever. After screaming themselves silly, a surge of humanity, the bulk of the audience, pummeled the bar with a thirsty vengeance. Flashing her ice green eyes to a few of the transfixed stragglers, she snapped the hard-shell case closed.

It had been a gift.

Just over thirty, with long dirty-blonde hair, Piper was a flower of feminine elegance. A natural splendor in ripped jeans and a tee-shirt, her lean frame gave the appearance of someone easily ten years her junior. There was a quizzical expression forever playing on her pouting lips, a soft wild smile.

Piper Wild was always hard not to stare at, but it was especially difficult after bearing witness to the fact that she could play guitar as few humans can. The gift was in the Wild family, she never had to learn, there'd been no prolonged process. One day she was a young girl and her Dad presented her with a toy guitar, the next day the toy made music.

Some did their homework, she joined a rock and roll band. Something inside demanded her true nature, her indelible identity, be expressed. There was no choice, it was not something Piper could let go of, and she'd tried.

She had to rock.

When she played, she fought for an equilibrium, for sanity. Now she was older, she knew the truth. She was fighting for her life.

That's what it is for some people. Definitely the way it was in the Wild family. As she left the stage, her guitar case in hand, she could hear her younger brother's laughter above the buzzing crowd and clamor of the club.

When he was three, thirty brats would be screaming their heads off. It's Buck you'd hear. That was what it was, he could just be heard.

The young, hauntingly attractive little brother of Piper Wild, he could sing like thundering velvet. His sound would grab your ear and not let go. She'd always known that voice was its own entity, like a living thing that resided within her brother, something he had, and would forever, live with.

Everett Wild, Jr., or Buck, as he'd always been called, was engaging, slender and sinewy, and just out of the starting gate at twenty-one. Highlighting his tight, lean, frame, the wife-beater he was wearing left his wide, sharp shoulders naked, a body just as powerful as his voice. Buck had inherited the proper name and athletic grace of their father, along with an endless potential for passion, sublime and savage.

The kid was a natural front-man, someone you wanted to watch. He was green, at his very beginning, but it was easy to understand what the audience had just seen in him. Rolling a cable, he was clearly charged from the energy of the set, and he strutted across to help Skyler pack up the drum kit.

Piper sauntered past the bar, accepting a long-neck bottle with her smile. The Wild was it. Just ripped the roof off, split this dump open, best band she'd ever played in.

People said things and touched her as she strode by.

Get me to the show. A guitar tech, a crew, and a battery of instruments to make props out of. With decent promotion and label support, we'll climb the charts, no doubts, this time it's all there.

Every suburban dead end has a breeding ground for musical punks, some small store stuck away in the corner of an old strip mall that every cool kid hangs around. Piper's early teens were spent working for Al Siren, owner/operator of Performance Music. Paying her in guitar strings, lessons, and when she turned sixteen with an old car, Siren had been a player, a tall, strange man who'd known her father when they were young.

After the store closed, Al started a home studio, cutting demos and independent albums for anyone who could hustle up some cash. When she had nowhere else to sleep she could always go to Al's, slip in the back of the studio and crash. Staying there and helping produce, Piper learned how to create a sound.

Everybody in the southend cut a demo at Star Lake Studios, or knew someone who did. Between the store and the studio, she was known enough that everyone wanted to jam with her, particularly all the young dudes. She learned to play guys as she played the guitar, like ringing a bell.

At fifteen she was already a player. Entranced by the bands of the day, so many boys, that only the grace of being a musician kept her this side of groupie. Everyone's little sister, people liked Piper, she partied and mingled with, her bands opened up for, local favorites, kids who would go on to develop into real recording artists, rock stars.

In the years to come, Piper would start several different bands, travel around the country, and see some of the world. She'd learn the business, land three recording deals of her own, make and blow a good-sized chunk of change. A decade and more peeled right on by, and the ups, downs, ins and outs of the business and lifestyle left her feeling far ahead and way behind of friends, neighbors, society, and life.

Cause and effect, who and what she'd chosen to be everyday of her life, she could live with it, whatever with the rest of the world. To her own self she'd always been true. What she was doing now was what it is, everything she'd learned, the best of what she had to offer.

Time, she could feel the cycle rolling on, the tick-tock
of the clock, and she wanted to fire back. She was striving for
more than another deal, or someone's idea of a large stack of
cash. After so many lessons in living, Piper now came to accept
the someone she had to be.

Walking up to her manager, Robert, she targeted the two
men standing next to him. One she'd met before, mid-thirties,
well groomed, overly hip in an expensive fashion. His friend
looked just the same.

These were guys from out of town, necktie or not,
company men with checkbooks, record label suits. They were
only here to catch this show. With one look in their eyes, she
knew they wanted to sign The Wild.

A mop of brown and graying curls, Robert was a quick-
talking, heavyset stump with thick black glasses who looked to
be approaching a real rough forty, at thirty-three. The sloppy
gravity with which he moved, and an aloof, conceited quality
made him seem like somebody's parent, or a principal. He did,
however, know how to talk to suits.

Buck was leaning against the foot of the stage, drinking
a beer with two young women in corduroy, and a large dude
with an arm and neck crowded with colorful tattoos. On
Buck's left shoulder, wearing a leather skirt and loud makeup, a
slim punker girl hung on him with a constant pinch and tickle.
One of the two corduroy women showered Buck in innuendo
and invitation, twirling a lasso of her long, jet-black hair

He responded kindly, taking down her number, saying he
would call when The Wild played again. A charmed sensuality
displaced most anybody's defenses and sex was always easy
for him, finding a partner and the act itself, fun. There was a
girlfriend since he could remember, it was systematic, the way
that part of his life was covered.

He was never much good at answering to anyone.

Buck figured some shrink would say he was looking to find the mother he never knew. Well, whatever, because if that was it, why he did what he did, then it was the best gift Mom left him, besides his voice. He was sincerely thankful, 'cause he made more tail than ten jackrabbits on shore leave.

Even as they moved on to other places and people, Buck remained on good terms with every girl, every person, he'd ever known. Some lost touch, but no one ever became an enemy. This touch for intimacy, tempered by tolerance, was part of his inherent understanding and wisdom.

Last call came and went, and the club calmed to near–closed. An avid single-mindedness encased Piper, Robert, and the suits in preliminary negotiations. Ready to go deal somewhere seriously, they finished their drinks and walked to the stage.

Everybody gathered around Buck, interrupting his current conversation, an exchange of numbers with jet-black corduroy. Skyler, with Bones the bass player in tow, came in from loading the van. Reading his older sister's smile, a chilled shiver raced over Buck's skin and Robert presented the band to the wide-eyed suits.

"Guys, let me introduce you to The Wild."

2

It was jet-black corduroy who had made the cut.

Clasping at his back with a deep and desperate need, her breath was thick with the smell of sweet liquor and flavored cigarettes. In the fleeting fervor of passion she pressed her body harder to Buck's. Seizing his lips, she whispered a prophecy.

"You're going to be a big star."

Her head lay on his chest, her corduroy on the floor. Buck removed a swath of black locks from his face, and peered up over the back of the couch, from beneath the thin, tattered blanket. Amps, cords, and music gear were everywhere.

The garage was their fortress, its walls a visual mosaic of personality; band shots, cutting from magazines, and a variety of pop-culture posters collided with a weird array of household artifacts. In the dim, distant corner, perched from the arm of a shredded blue chair, Bones was rapt in earnest concentration. He intermediately took drags off his left hand and slugs of beer from his right, listening intently as Sky set up his drums and slanged some rap.

Bones was a serious bass player and an even more committed rocker. Twenty-one gangly years old, he earned his nickname at a much earlier age, the skinny kid a full head higher than his peer group. His real name was Jeffery Pine, an only child, always tall and slender and angular, with distinctive features and an undeniable affability.

Buck began to jam with Bones after sixth grade band, and when Jeff's mom, seeing some blackened bruises on his forearms and neck, asked Buck to stay with them, he did, all the way through high school. The only reason Buck graduated, wasn't on the street, or who knows where else, was the stability and acceptance he'd found in the Pine family, a sane and sober environment. Bones and Buck, or Jeff and Everett Jr., were the kind of friends who shared such a similar sense of life and laughter, being and humor, that they finished each other's sentences, brothers thicker than blood.

Against the express commandment of his parents, and to the awe of his classmates, Bones had showed up at fourteen with an arm full of tattoo.

An expansive technicolor rose, the flower on his shoulder, vibrant red petals and three green-black leaves, gave way to a jagged stem that wrapped around his long thin bicep and down his forearm, ending in a painted bracelet of thorn. He'd worn long sleeves for two weeks while the work was done, and it would have cost a bundle if he hadn't gotten this older hippie chick, known as the Big Girl, to do it for free.

Bones got most everything for free, usually it was girls he knew, who worked places, that gave him gifts. Bones's family was truly middle class, actual dysfunction could be found over at Buck's house. To appease his parents and extend his slack time shelf-life, he attended community college, dogging chicks and playing bass, wanting nothing more out of life.

Suddenly, Sky paused in his rhetoric, straining his ear to hear tires land on the gravel of the driveway outside.

"Who's that? That ain't their old man is it?"

Skyler turned out the light. Jumping across the room, Bones peeked out a covered window. After a moment of deliberation, he shouted a declaration of safety.

"It's Piper and Robert."

A wave of relief hit the room, and Buck poked his head up from the couch.

"Open the door."

Piper could be heard before she was seen. "Studio time is booked, kids."

She rushed in, flipping on the main overhead lights with Robert following closely, his usual slow plod quickened to a sloppy strut.

With a collective shout out, they all gathered around the couch, Bones behind, Piper and Skyler sitting together on the arm. Buck and his guest scrambled under the blanket, assembling the corduroy and then themselves. Robert barked in a sober and commanding tone.

"Meeting, my office, tomorrow at two, then the label is taking us all out to lunch."

Buck's arms shot into the air. "Free lunch."

Piper jolted into a pace, a fierce fire in her eyes, just all business.

"Ok, look here kids, this is where the work starts."

Her impending speech was cut short by another car hitting the gravel driveway.

"It's Everett, hit the lights."

Behind the windshield, the lights going out in the garage were a blurred insult. Slowly fumbling around to turn the static of the radio off, his drunken arm, swaying with hesitation, tipped a bottle up delivering a long pull. Then the arm and the bottle fell to the front seat, passed out.

Practice pads cost cash, the room had a good sound, and with Buck staying at home again, it seemed possible to use the garage. It worked for a while, got the band a good start, but it

15

was clear now they needed to move. Peeping from the garage to the car, Piper could hear the engine's chopping rumble.

With his own income and feeling full grown, Buck had moved back home because he thought it was what he should do. The old man sobered up some, or seemed to, and pled for him to stay there. A tough deliberation, but Buck took the opportunity, perhaps his only chance to connect, before his father was too far gone.

He wanted some relationship, and if he could to maybe help, if possible. To stay, to go, it all seemed set against him, but Buck was always brave and you take a chance when one presents itself. So he'd been home for the last six months or so.

Staying with Everett was tough on her brother. But if he wanted to reconnect, who was she to say different? The two shared more than just a name, she figured Buck best understand his father to know himself.

Some problems are hard to leave behind, even when you left them at thirteen. A hundred years ago she'd split school and ran from here, from this very spot. Piper wondered at the weird round trip that brought her back here now, a tear in her eye, as she stared out at her father's still idling Cadillac.

Everett had made it home again.

3

Lighting a fresh smoke from the remains of his current butt, Robert threw the burning filter out his window as they swerved up the freeway on-ramp.

"Piper, the label's already cut a check for studio time, we'll negotiate based on what they hear."

"If they don't bite?"

"They have right of first refusal, after ninety days it's ours." Their rap was the rhythm of business and they loved it.

Having been to the dance before, Piper knew the game and the lingo. Robert owned a certain audacity that comes from a budding confidence and real ambition.

"They're gonna bite. They're gonna swallow." "Yeah?"

"PartyGirl is a legend, their whole staff are huge fans of Diary, and Clark and his man love the Wild, they really freaked when they saw Buck."

Now that was much too cocky, thought Piper. He's going to jinx the whole deal. The guarded skepticism of her response demanded more information.

"Freaked?"

"Made a phone call right then, said get them in the studio, now, this is it, The Wild. Piper, they're talking about a bus."

"Already?"

"Test you with some support slots, open for a few of the big boys, kids from your old gang."

She let his last comment hang in the air, as her head was already somewhere else. Think about it. Break it down again.

The Wild hadn't released anything independent, a single, nothing. This was her first band in two years and they'd only played six shows, three of those had been out of town. Buck had only been in one band before this and they never even played out at all.

But here we are getting attention from the majors. Wait, that's not so crazy, we started the groundwork more than a decade ago, way before The Wild was ever even imagined. Organizing her racing thoughts, she glanced to the sight of Robert chewing down yet another cigarette.

Fifteen minutes before first period, smoking pot out of a pop can across the street from the school, behind the trees, next to an enormous boulder painted thick with graffiti, that's where all the cool kids started their morning back in junior high. How far this overweight chimney sitting next to her had come since then, how much they'd been through. Robert had been hustling the whole time.

Robert was the first contemporary of Piper's that really saw the whole picture. Early on he was packaging, planning and mailing things off to people and places. Most of all, he talked on the phone.

He started by setting up a series of battle of the bands, and then shows at halls and lodges, and notoriously at the local Skate King. He was one of those few shakers that turned the scene into a big deal, got the radio to talk about local bands, made tee-shirts, flyers and promotions, and when the shows sold out, he took a nice cut of the door. Collecting demos, Robert proposed to manage bands he liked and thought he could pitch to the major leagues.

There was no number he wouldn't dial, no voice he couldn't engage. Always professional and courteous, he was mainly persistent and repetitious. He'd turn one call into four contacts, and by the end of every day there were more numbers, names, dates, and figures scrawled into his book.

Robert's debut battle of the bands was won by PartyGirl. Overnight he had them playing all over the area. They retained quite a following, these five hot teenage girls in ripped leather that could actually play.

PartyGirl had been Piper's second group, and first real band. Cry Vandal, like the effort Buck had just disbanded, was basically garage rock guitar school. In PartyGirl, she sang backup vocals and played lead guitar.

The lead singer, Debby, was the only rich kid in the band. Her father partially owned a large paper company and a lot of real estate. On one such hunk of land, deep in the southernmost bowels of the suburbs, lost behind overgrown brambles, and weathered with over twenty years of desertion, sat an old farmhouse.

It was a three-story structure fashioned after a quasi-Victorian floor plan, built in the early twenties, when the present-day bustling burbs were the way-out sticks. One of the first homes of its stature to grace the landscape so far south of the city, the grounds were now overgrown with blackberries. Old Douglas fir trees blocked its view from most of the world.

Without the cultural guidance of a tradition generations old, things can become eccentric, unique, if not odd, and the house, built like most of the Northwest, had borrowed eclectically and kept what worked. The lines were mostly traditional, but the roof slanted steep, the windows strangely boxy, and despite the rounded, elegant pillars and the large southern-style sitting porch, it echoed the sight of a log cabin with a thyroid problem.

When the entire band took up residence in the beaten old structure, it was so weathered as to be questionably livable, in a serious state of dilapidation and disrepair, abandoned for several decades. Within a few short months it came to be known as the Tramp House. Legendary was the action, huge and frequent bashes punctuated the rock and roll that endured all night, the party that was everyday.

Just over two years they reigned as queens. After each PartyGirl show the house became stuffed to capacity with liquor, music, and love. Born to party, the way they lived.

With the electric bill being the only major drag, the power was off half the time. Huge fires would be lit in the oversized stone fireplace to compensate. The dark and decay of the structure gave the worn cavernous house an endless and haunting feel.

The Tramp House could host a crazed collection of different parties at the same time. Each girl had taken a room and made it livable, to one degree or another, and small gatherings would be strayed throughout the place. Upstairs, an intimate coke-fueled orgy might be fully underway while a bunch of beer-soaked interlopers played Ping-Pong two floors down.

After one particularly well-attended show, Debby invited the entire audience back to the house again, and most came. It was so far from any neighbors or the main road that cars had to fill the long driveway, and the vacant field in front of the house, before overflow parking would start on the highway. This is what would attract the authorities.

Many times the driveway was lined with vehicles while cops directed traffic and people left in droves. A section of the party would bail into the woods, which surrounded the house, and wait for the pigs to leave. When they did, the party would start all over again.

But the last night the Tramp House stood, the cops showed up after the fire department. The fervor of the party was sparked to violence when a crafty underground entrepreneur code-named the General casually cast a bottle from the middle of the crowd in the front yard. His empty shattered into the bay window on the front of the home, spraying glass about with an deafening crash.

A startled moment of silence followed the sound of the shatter, a brief pause before crazed frenzy broke loose and took hold. Anything that could be picked up was thrown at and into the house. Inside a mob ripped, broke, and bashed.

The stone fireplace was stoked until flames leapt for freedom. Fire ran up and down the halls and the walls. When the department finally put it out, Debby's dad had a list of litigation and the party was over.

Debby was sent to a prep school, another girl got pregnant, and out of the ashes came a three-piece group named Diary.

This time Piper took the vocals and lead guitar. Better gigs came right away, and so did a record deal.

Robert had a knack of getting the right people to see the right show. When Bernie Goldman, head of a major label, not just some A&R working stiff, saw Diary play at a rough little club by the waterfront, under the freeway and attached to an old dive hotel, he wasted no time. The rush was on for the sound, a few local bands had already been picked up, and he wasn't going to let anybody steal Diary.

Bernie signed Diary and soon the girls were out in a van. Piper made a publishing deal, pocketing a nice hunk of cash, gig after gig got better and soon the van became a bus. Four drummers, two albums, and several years later, she had received industry notice and some artistic praise.

She'd made it to the show.

The wind changed, the world turned, and Bernie Goldman lost his job. A man named Pinkerton chaired the label now, and he had a whole new agenda, including an all-girl band his niece was in. With Pinkerton in charge, the label's interest and backing waned from Diary, the good support shows, the networking push, the money and resources, all went to the niece and the rest of Pinkerton's bitches.

Robert and Piper learned it was all politics and timing. It had nothing to do with Piper, or Diary, not being great. They had a loyal following, toured the country constantly, and were getting picked up on college radio everywhere.

Diary got cut from the label, and it devastated Piper, she'd never felt so disconnected from herself, so lost, like something abruptly scooped away the magic that had always made her special. The music, the life and game, was her fantasy, where she was a super-hero, where she could do no wrong, where she couldn't be touched, a rocker, a big talker with a finger in your face. When cold reality crashed the illusion it was a major blow.

The old story of faded glory, at twenty-something she was used product.

She dropped out of view, disappeared, could have gone to the moon, nobody would have known. There was no phone, home, or anything to tie her to the world. Cut loose from the responsibility of a band, the only real grounding force she'd known, Piper went as close to crazy as she'd ever let herself get.

It was her father's story that hounded her, the shadow of her own. A single-hit sensation, a one-time talent that didn't get enough time. Inheriting broken dreams is bad enough, but to bust your own, that might break you.

After everything, every gig, flophouse and practice pad, the demos, albums, interviews and meetings, important calls and all the craziness, when she wanted to walk away, in every instance she had simply consoled herself with the sound. It'd

marked her, and in her mind she needed to find what was the
original joy, the words and music, her guitar, something inside
that she'd tried, but would not let her go. She wanted to lose
the things that were her, and for six months she didn't even
touch a guitar.

Robert had even engineered a beautiful payoff when they
got dumped. But cash didn't help, somehow it made it worse,
so she spent, blew through it all, duck-farts and micro-beers,
hotel rooms and good coke. Soon she was selling her guitars.

She went to a lot of cities she'd only seen from a bar and
a bus, she hung out at with some friends in NY for a while,
hitched the coast and got lost into Cape Fear, spent a week in
Florida once, and month with a farm-boy from Kansas, who
lived in Tennessee. She loved to hitchhike, a new adventure
with every brake-light and open door. It was always easy for her
to get a ride, almost anyone would want to pick her up. maybe
even more so. Sister grunge with a small backpack and a smile,
beautiful and free. The only real baggage she ever bore was in
her mind and memory.

Down to just her Gretch, a pig-nose amp, and thirty-
some bucks, Piper hopped a Greyhound from Portland
and headed home. For a week she slept in the park over the
Freeway, played for change at the Market. Soon she was staying
at a friend's practice pad in Georgetown.

And what was she supposed to do now? Piper saw that at
a certain point you only got the guns you gave yourself, and she
felt ruined for any regular job, or some straight life she'd never
lived. Bernie Goldman had given her a check for seven songs
larger than anyone she'd known growing up made in seven
years, for seven songs.

Being lost and found and finally coming around, she
knew she wanted another shot. She'd been paid, had lived,
tasted the life of a rock star. Some she'd come up with had
made the sound into a mountain of gold.

Part of her felt the industry, the game, the music itself owed. She had a payday coming, no nickels and no dimes, the motherload, the whole life and style. But she also knew the odds, the insane numbers between her and what she had already accomplished, let alone what she might be able to manifest in the future; but what the hell, heroes often fail.

The thought flashed a succession of circumstance from the past, and she reminded herself it's a game, we play for fun, for life and love. Too many didn't make it this far for her to get wrapped up into chasing the great golden donut, long ago she learned to stay cool and embrace what was of real importance. A song came to her ear and the shape of a familiar face flooded her mind.

Many miles away, like a madman dream, she remembered a friend and lover, a singer, local rocker, that had caught an early cab from the needle, and her smile softened as she felt the tears for someone long gone. A song he used to sing played in her head, it begged the question, what's one to do? Play like there is no tomorrow, that's what you do.

She wiped the wet steam from her window. Rolling it down a crack, the cold freeway drizzle blew in on her face. They rounded the last curve to the city, the road mist eased and a bright gray glare lit the approaching view of Seattle.

The city was a whole lot more than it used to be. Perhaps better, worse, and all the things in-between, but it was indisputably bigger, taller, and brighter. Coming up the I-5 it looked like some modern day version of Rome, winding roads and mammoth sports stadiums, towers of glass demonstrating power and prosperity.

A place of invention, Piper figured that's what it was. That people came, still do, from everywhere, to populate the one corner of the country that hadn't been neck-deep in people since current history could remember. Even gentrified with wealth she saw the spine of the old city.

Exiting the freeway and heading into Seattle, she watched Robert inhale a cloud of smoke and couldn't help visualize the real Skid Row. A phrase coined here, right here, she thought, as they exited I-5. Logs from the hill 'skidded' downhill to the waterfront in a 'row,' towards the great Puget Sound and the world market.

Gateway to the great north, to adventure, and gold. The bluest skies you've ever seen lofting over a pioneer settlement surrounded by lakes, rivers, and enormous mountains. Sailors, loggers, and such, that was when it was a port town, with a little bit of all the world in it. Watch your mouth and cover your ass.

The Wild children were reared to be Northwest history buffs. Piper even dated a guy who gave tours of the Seattle Underground. She'd given Buck his nickname from her favorite book, read to her as a kid, Call of the Wild.

How much Seattle had changed from when she'd first gigged downtown. More than not those places no longer existed. shirts with slogans like: "Hey, I sold-out in Belltown."

The southend is where she'd been raised. The burbs. Federal Way, Washington, about sixteen miles south of Seattle.

FW is the embodiment of suburban sprawl. An endless maze of unplanned roads and franchised chains. Her whole life Piper watched the woods get ripped down, replaced with cheap apartments, gas stations, and strip-malls, more people, more scars upon the land.

Was there ever a place that grew up so quickly?

Like all of modern day America, it kept growing until it exaggerated into an obscene obesity. Fed-LA is what the kids called it now. And as much of it that didn't resemble any of the places she remembered, when she drove there lately to practice, in spite of herself, she knew it was where she was from.

It was a revolving door since she was very young. Piper loved her father, but he'd been drowning in the bottle before she could recall. That made many things difficult.

But now, now, it was redemption for everyone, even for Everett. By letting them use the garage, and spotting some cash for a decent PA, he was a part of this. Catch him before he was wasted and he'd tell you himself what it meant for him to see his kids, to hear them play.

The songs they'd worked were sharp and radio-friendly, yet edgy. Together the band produced a genius that was undeniably unique, fact was they were as twice as hot as hell on Sunday. No small wonder Clark and his man at the label freaked.

The Wild was the one, she knew it was.

4

An afternoon burst of sunlight split the sky's canopy of gray and partially lit the lot they were parked in.

It was shortly before two, and the boys were sitting in a beat-up dark blue Dodge Colt passing a pipe. They were listening to their demo over and over with a zealous intensity.

Skyler was in the driver's seat, Bones the passenger, and Buck sat in the back.

The three-song demo, recorded in the Wild's garage, got devoured by the city's musical elite. Piper's reputation, Robert's connections, the quality of the work all brought the suits to the show. Combining many years of working in garages and basements with her experience in professional and hi-end studios, Piper had learned to finagle with endless amounts of mixing boards, condensers, mikes, and the like, to render a production and sound of an unusual quality on a shoestring.

It had the sharp edge of upper-end audio production, while retaining the warm, rough, tube sound that some producers pay big bucks and inflict pain to emulate. The Wild had written scores of songs in the short time they were together. Picking three for the demo was a difficult task.

Piper made everyone aware whatever they put down had to be instantly marketable, musically viable, and showcase an enormous future potential. These weren't the days when any jerk could get a record deal. Most prospective bands had to already have it going on.

A band needed to be established and already enjoy a fan base. It was standard stuff to have several independent releases, a web-site with impressive traffic, and so on. A million kids learned to play three chords and turned themselves into self-promotion machines since she'd plugged in.

The first two songs were instantly familiar, catchy anthem rock hardened with more hooks than a tackle box. Bones and Sky fused tight, unrelenting rhythms with offbeat timing in an unusual way, simple and appealing. Piper mixed traditional progressions with spiked fills, breaks and her soaring leads.

Weaving his voice and lyrics in and around the band, Buck harnessed a quality all timeless music has; it could be no other way. What other music would fit with that voice? How lonely the voice would be without that sound.

The third cut on the demo was Smile Child, the only song brother and sister had written together. Buck wrote the verses, like all the band's lyrics, but Piper had taught him this rhyme when he was a kid. The chorus was a lullaby she had written with her mother as a young girl.

'Smile child, prayer for the wild, sing me a song, make the smile shine a while.'

Musically Piper thought it was her best work, the orchestration was dynamic enough to envelop clean harmonies, a pop-ish melancholy melody, and the appealing crunch of an ass-kicking punk hook. It was a signature song complete with a sing-along chorus. It defined The Wild, the manner and approach to the music they played, what would become their style.

Every ear heard the dollar signs of a crossover hit.

"It's got the feeling of a long time friend you just met." Skyler took a blast from a small brass pipe and held the pull as he continued to speak.

"Rocks, it rocks, rocks, rocks . . . listen here."

To illustrate his point, Sky pushed the speakers to distortion, then snagged a toke again, passing the bowl back. Buck inhaled quick, as to not let the cherry go out, and then lidded the pipe with his thumb. Pressing his cheeks out, he bobbed slightly, then exploded in a cloud of smoke.

"Who's not gonna want to sing-a-long to that?"

Skyler joined in with the chorus, emphasizing the beat with sharp strikes to the steering wheel. Bones claimed the bowl from Buck, who handed it off absently amongst an ardent attack of coughing. Turning the tune to a low roar, Bones ripped at the weed, and then snorted over the music to Sky.

"Hey, man, isn't that Robert a fat bastard snake in the grass?"

"Yes, but he is our fat bastard snake in the grass."

Sky spoke with the confident tones of a scholar. "A band is a band, but business is business."

Bones's exhaling smoke mingled with his words, his question was a rasp.

"So, everybody needs a good snake?"

"That's right, just leave it all to Piper, she knows more about this than we do."

Emptying the ash out the window into the soft wind coming up from Lake Union, Sky tapped the bowl against the side of the Colt, then stashed the brass under the floor mat. The song finished and Skyler mused in a seriously stoned pontification.

"Playing in a band is just like a fishing trip. Getting out of town, driving, camping, all the whatnot and accompanying chaos, you only get a fraction of time to actually play, or fish, or whatever."

A pause hung in the air, then the demo began to play again, and Bones lit a smoke. Buck sang softly along with the song, and as it built he began kicking at the seat in rhythm. Brushing hair back from his eyes, Skyler glanced to the rearview mirror.

"Here they are."

Watching Robert and Piper pull into the parking lot, Sky gave his head a shake and wrestled the key from the ignition. "That's good grass."

Passing out a pack of gum between them, Bones, Buck and Skyler all climbed out of the Colt. They marched up to Robert's car with a palatable anticipation. Sky opened Piper's door for her, and as she stepped out she gave a whisper to his ear.

"How's it going?"

The two walked a few paces away for a moment of privacy. He touched her smile with the tips of his fingers. Quickly, they enwrapped, locking in a kiss.

With the build and appearance more of a preppy than a rocker, Skyler shone like America's golden son. Guilty of being from an upper-upper-class home, he'd been a track and field star before dropping out of high school. When his parents found some weed in his room, there was an intervention and Sky moved out for good.

It was the height of hypocrisy for his parents to have attempted to intervene into anything. Sky knew his father's silver spoon was often filled with coke. He watched Mother do a daily pickling of herself with beautiful bottles of expensive vodka.

A hand was never laid on Skyler, that was the problem.

He'd grown up in the distinctly distant arms of the rich. His upbringing had forced Sky to furnish himself with a world of his own.

"He's got a good head but he just don't apply it."

After being asked to leave three private institutions, his parents finally relented and let Skyler attend public school. All his teachers said just the same as before. He talks too much, is hyperactive, disturbs other students, underachieves in most areas.

Far brighter then any faculty member he was ever introduced to, Skyler James the Third's inheritance would be exponentially greater than the combined yearly salaries of a district full of public school teachers, and he knew it. A combination of looks, youth, and a distinct disdain for his own wealth led him to an instant contempt for anyone claiming authority in any fashion. It was simply in Sky to rebel, challenge and provoke.

His old man had inherited from the family legacy, sat on the board of several banks, drove a Ferrari, always traveled a lot, and now kept several mistresses about Sky's age. Mom was a selfless part of the community, she sat on multiple boards and committees, and gave to organizations that helped the less fortunate. Then from mid-morning on, she drank.

Sky had two older sisters that were perfect. Both sisters, the youngest his senior by nine years, had gone to proper schools and done all the right things, gone to college, married, and now had kids of their own. Clearly marked as the black sheep, Sky was an obvious accident, the family afterthought, and by the age of three his Mom knew he was way too much for her to manage.

Growing up it was impossible to keep clothes on the boy, and even as a young man he didn't like to wear shirts, in fact he was most comfortable without anything on. He always played the drums barefoot and half naked. Part of it was a vanity, pride in such a taut and physically perfect form, but there was an element of the inability for anything to wrap, encapsulate, or capture him, nothing was allowed to ever hold, censor, or impede.

He had a soft voice, and a quiet beauty that portrayed him as shy to those who didn't know him. A curious expression, an ever-skeptical smirk seldom left his face. Skyler was a person who would never fear the hammer of any consequence.

When he split from his folks' house in Marine Hills, Sky left stacks of unworn v-neck sweaters, turtlenecks, chinos, and expensive shoes piled in his room. After slamming the door, he'd still show up for birthdays and holidays, but never took the cash they offered, and would leave any gifts. He'd laugh at his sisters' mention of college, and thank them for their concern.

The street kid game was fun for him. Sky was always everybody's instant buddy and he slept around, staying in a parade of flops and street dives, with his perfect teeth. Nothing ever seemed to bother him, as he had no expectations.

He fell into rock and roll. A friend let him crash out in a practice pad. After witnessing a loud and band-ending argument that resulted in a small scuffle and an ousted drummer, Sky calmly reported to the remaining members that he played the drums, and indeed he did.

If they'd needed a pianist, someone to tap dance or fence, he could do that too. Lessons, Mother had put little Skyler in every class possible from the day she had a name to register. Finding the family in his band that he hadn't accepted anywhere else, and coupled with a natural compulsion to hit things, playing drums became Skyler's favorite thing to do.

Led Feet played the local clubs for several years, releasing three independent albums, and were featured on several independent film soundtracks. They opened up for a couple national acts, support slots for a few European tours, and packed a club every couple weeks on their own. They made enough bread to pay for their manager's phone bill, and retain their rehearsal room.

Passed out at that practice pad is where Piper first laid eyes on Skyler. She was supposed to meet a mutual friend to jam, and showed up early. There he was, curled up on a couch at the foot of an amplifier, a sight that made her laugh.

The old warehouse, cut into many shoebox-sized practice rooms, was a most peculiar place for anyone to get some shuteye. But there Sky was, soundly sawing it off, amid the rock and racket that thundered throughout the derelict studios. She watched him sleep, struck with an intense feeling of familiarity.

An instant intimacy kindled the moment he woke. Even though Sky was four years younger, they were a perfect couple. The cynical distance his worldly experience had lent him matched the hardened wisdom her struggle had gifted her.

When Led Feet broke up around the time Piper was looking to put together a new band, it just sort of happened. She seldom saw anyone so avid in his playing, he chewed through drumsticks with perfect meter. After seeing him exclusively for a while, Piper was surprised herself, when he became the drummer of The Wild.

Skyler had a natural energy that elevated the confidence of anyone around him, and Buck's mannerisms and speech began to mirror Sky's in a short amount of time. The chemistry couldn't be denied. Bones instantly connected with him and the bass became bedrock with the beat.

As the sun disappeared behind a towering glass building, Robert, garbed in his best black tee-shirt, issued clear instructions on that darkening gray day.

"Here's how it goes, everybody clams up. Let me and Piper do all the talking."

Powered by the lucid calm of a fresh bake, Buck placed a pair of cheap sunglasses on the bridge of his nose.

"Just happy to be here."

5

Mornings were the worst on Everett, so he scheduled all his appointments in the early afternoon.

This gave him time to put himself together, have a quick couple shots before a short shower, make a few phone calls.

He'd leave messages at the office and with clients to prove to the world he was up and running, perhaps even busy that morning, and then make it out the door half-dressed and still shaving with his electric.

One of his favorite things was to stop in to meet some buddies in the a.m. for a few libations. In the evenings and afternoons, he frequented a rotation of bars, lounges, and taverns. The old school establishments, dives that had been around, independently owned places with character were his favorites.

But in the mornings, it was either the bowling alley or Diamond Jack's. They were both close enough to be home, opened early for drinks, and it was a toss-up as to which was his favorite. His special brand of bull, his ability to roll, and an indescribable endurance for alcohol had made him a legend.

He was given to impulse and emotion, and something in his nature was forever reckless. His character was to become increasingly exaggerated and engaging, with additional shots and beers, right up until he became the derelict fool, and then the dangerous drunk. One of those people who got lucky when they were inebriated, he'd win more pull-tabs, split more pins, make more women than reasonable odds would seem to dictate possible.

Somebody had said something about something he'd recently done at the alley, and he couldn't remember who said it, or exactly what had been said, but he thought it best to stay clear of there for a little while. He had bits, partial snippets, of some memories that might be what they were talking about, and none of it seemed good. It had been at least a week since he'd been in, and the thing he thought most curious was that he couldn't find his bowling ball anywhere, so just wondering what might have happened made him edgy.

Everett Wild had always moved with a relaxed confidence and strength. A striking and athletic man in his early fifties, he had features that had verged on pretty in his youth. Smooth in speech and demeanor, his energy and physical vocabulary lived on the edge of mischief, if not violence.

Now the jagged scars of his soul were written on his face, and bottling himself for so long, his skin was tightening to leather. Some fellas get sloppy fat and bloated like his drinking buddy Frank, but the years had proved that Everett was the kind of boozer that only hardened with abuse. When he did eat, it wasn't much, maybe a late-night chili dog and a beer.

Pulling into the parking lot of a single-story, simple brick building, the dark green Cadillac, his personal office and mobile motel, was rounded at the corners and running with a raspy chug, one step away from being a complete junker. If parked on the other side of a lot, if it was raining out, or dark, it still clung to an air of respectability, but close up it was obviously weathered, just like Everett.

Affixed above the front door, a neon sign reading
'Cocktails' bathed the entrance in blood red. Back in its day,
it was a slightly upscale steak house, and the name Diamond
Jack's was painted in decorative gold on the front door. The
lettering had long since faded to a flat yellow.

A classic slice of the American alcoholic, Diamond
Jack's was a dingy, windowless pit frequented by an assorted
mix of mid-to-low level businessmen, engineers, drug dealers,
divorcees, reasonably priced hookers, riffraff and regulars.
Protected by a bubble of alcohol and smoke, it could be
anytime of day or night and it stayed the same sparsely filled
den of booze and slurring babble. This was Everett's favorite
time to be here, middle of the morning, late enough not to be
early, but early enough to still have a day ahead.

High-backed black, synthetic leather booths surrounded
the perimeter of the room. Dim candles, glowing in small red
jars, sat on top of a few round cocktail tables with swiveling
black bucket chairs before them.

Someone had affixed the beautifully ornate wooden bar
with a vinyl padded rail, and bottles, taps, glasses, and pull tab
boxes now obstructed the full-length mirror behind it.

It was a place best described as a lounge.

Despite how sociable he seemed, Everett felt the creep of
loneliness, more so in a crowded room. The bottle, his oldest
friend, had always been there for him. It could beat the creep,
block it out.

He couldn't say the booze didn't get in the way, sure he
felt rough in the morning, and yeah, he probably did a lot of
things he wouldn't do otherwise. But who doesn't? No matter
how late the night, he never missed a day of work, not one.

Dragged his ass around daily to deal with clients and
contracts, made it into the office twice a week, paid his bills,
his taxes, hadn't caused a ruckus in a long while, least not a big

one. Everett figured by the time a man did all that he deserved to drink. Hell, drinking was part of his job.

Half his clients he met in bars. The other half he took there to do business, discuss issues, come to terms, continue relationships, and cultivate prospects. Everything he did went with a drink, everything he'd always done.

The day bartender at Diamond Jack's was Del, a portly hobbit with an infectious laugh. Del carried a section of newspaper, a half-glass of tomato juice, and a pint of draft beer, placing all three before Everett. He then turned to pour a shot.

Elbow propped against the edge of the bar as to steady his aim, Everett's hand was shaking slightly as he slowly filled the juice glass with the beer.

Del placed the shot in front of Everett, who threw it back with his free hand while continuing to create his special mix. Then he drank about half his red-beer in a gulp and opened the paper. Without looking up from the sports section, Everett tapped the shot-glass, a cue for Del to pour.

Everett hammered the second shot without looking up from the paper.

"Miami covered my spread."

Gambling was a lounge past-time. He never watched the games and didn't care much for sports, not since music had taken him away from the play-field to the honky-tonk when he was young. Who won what ballgame was a conversation piece, now a part of business, like drinking.

Del finished pouring a drink for a middle-aged woman seated around the corner, three stools up from Everett. She was dressed simply in a black skirt and print blouse. The lipstick was a little too red, her hair in need of another dye job, and she bore the rosy complexion of a consummate barfly.

Returning to Everett with a third shot, Del recognized the wry smile on Everett's face, predicting the question.

"Hey, Del, what's the story here?"

Wiping the bar, Del looked up and gave a wink. It prompted Everett to pick up his drink and saunter over to the woman. His confident stride culminated with a sly smile.

"Mind if I bum a smoke?"

She stiffened in response, but her eyes didn't leave her drink.

"Pardon?"

The coy response pleased Everett and he took the seat next to her, pulling the stool closer to the bar, closer to her. "A cigarette, may I have one?"

She slid him the package of smokes sitting before her, and he pulled one from the pack, tapping it uniformly on the bar. "And then he asked me for a light."

Engaged by the game, Everett volleyed in earnest. "What's that?"

"That's how I'll tell the story later on. I was sitting at Diamond Jack's when my knight in shining armor bummed a smoke, and then asked me for a light."

Venturing an amused sigh, she was pleased with her retort, the sardonic charm with which it was delivered. Everett shot down the rest of his drink. Then he slammed the glass down on the bar with a loud knock.

"Hey Del, another round for the lady and me please, and a pack of matches, huh?"

Del walked back with the drinks and the matches. Everett tapped the smoke on the bar, gazing at the side of her face. Setting the glasses down and lighting Everett up, Del left the matchbook behind.

She stirred, staring into her new drink. The smoke was a one-hundred, or a long smoke, and Everett tore the filter off, placing it in the ashtray. Pulling in an overstated drag, he spoke with the exhale.

"Filthy habit."

She parried without looking at him. "Why do you do it?"

"Fills a need."

He took a pack from his own pocket, presenting them with purpose.

"See, now, these are mine. Full flavor, straights, what you have there are menthols. I feel like something exotic."

After a quick flirt with hesitation, she lifted the fresh drink to her lips. Then, picking a smoke out of his pack, slowly she licked the filter. Turning to him, the smoke found her fire red lipstick and she looked directly into Everett's eyes for the first time.

"Got a light?

6

Wearing a long white leather coat, purple glasses, and a ribbon in her hair, Piper sat in a corner chair.

The private upstairs nook of this Capitol Hill coffeehouse was adorned with rustic wood paneling, expensive Northwest carvings, a wall display of a local watercolor artist, and towering shelves stacked with old books; to her left, a floor length window framed the overcast drizzle of the city, to her right Robert was sneaking a smoke in this non-smoking section, in front of her was a bright-eyed, pudgy, mid-twenties lesbian with a face full of piercings, a large coffee drink, and a notebook full of enthusiastic questions. Piper's chair gave a creak as her knee-high black boots propped up on the window ledge, her back against the wall.

Cool as cool could be, when she was under any spotlight, an icy edge accompanied her speech, demeanor, and movements. Feeling the cage of any question, Piper learned to think first, think again, then answer deliberately. Sometimes it is wise for a person with opinions to hold their tongue, and like most everything else, she'd learned that the hard way.

That is why Robert was representing, he respected Piper for her views and convictions and so on, sure, but didn't need any issues cropping up between him and a record deal. Got something to say, say it in your song or shut up, that's the way he saw it, and said so openly. He'd been clear with the local music editor of this rag that they wanted softball lobs, fan based stuff, no questions concerning anything other than The Wild.

He'd met the pudgy pierce-faced reporter, an exuberant fan of Piper's named Claire, a week before the interview and agree on what would be asked. A transplant from somewhere in the Midwest, she was pumped to meet, let alone interview, Piper Wild. Armed with a degree in journalism, Claire moved out west to be accepted, to find love and work, but really she came because of the music.

It was everything in the world for her to be writing this piece. Before Claire left college, she'd circled Seattle with a permanent black marker on a map. Now, everyday she woke up and thought, here I am, how about that.

Tracking down everything Piper ever recorded, she listened incessantly, reserved this room at the coffeehouse, and showed up fifteen minutes early. A single wave from the sea of youth that crashed on the shores of the Sound, Claire had come to the city looking for something genuine. Today she met a legend.

In a lot of Claire-like, hyper-punk, ultra-swank circles, Piper was as hip as it can get. She'd been close enough to smell the cigar, but never canned and served up for the masses. The underground appeal and localization of her notoriety rendered her recognized, the living embodiment of a spectacular scene.

Piper remained pure as an animal still in the wild.

"Your latest effort seems to target a wide appeal. A lot of folks might say you're starting to go pop."

"That's horsefeathers."

It'd been awhile since Piper had done this, and her own quick answer called a smile to her face. The abrupt edge of

Piper's response ruffled pudgy Claire. A tougher course came with the next question.

"As you get older, do you find it difficult to keep going with the same intensity that marked your earlier work?"

Robert shifted, looking to Piper with a slight concern.

"What is cool is to be at the beginning of something, you know?"

Piper launched into an articulate answer speaking of time, culture and music with an insight and eloquence that almost lost the college grad.

Everywhere she went, there she was, Piper Wild, and people would ask her about it. Where, what, when, why, all that bull. She'd shut down anyone who ran their mouth too much, but for the most part it was a sea of friends and admirers happy to know someone who had been to the show.

You're a bartender, an aerospace mechanic, or an adhesive salesman, few folk inquire much past the title of your post. Play rock and roll, your life is everybody's topic, and some people's target. Let's talk about what you've done, what you are doing, and what you're going to do.

Things she'd done, places and people, it was mystical to some folk, and she understood that. But she'd been there, where and when and what she was doing, the whole time. She thought simple action separated her, that it had been a clear equation of putting in, learning and building, action and result.

I play guitar, a drummer, there's a bass, someone sings, sell tickets and people show, give you money, that's actuality. Do a demo, that's a recording, play it, listen to it, share with a friend, it's irrefutable, period. We're a band, this is music, like it or hate it, ignore it, whatever, it's been made part of reality, this is tangible, this is real.

In their eyes, she could see people's need for a dream, their demand for a hero. When she wasn't climbing to the top anymore, without radio play, she felt the ice of their anger. Like a lottery ticket that didn't pay, mad, they'd be mad with their disappointment in the lost faith and energy they'd invested into to her.

It was as though she'd made her friends, family, and fans all fools, by association and default. She could see that they felt like suckers for every shirt they'd bought. They'd dared to tell friends about the band, had spent time listening to and following an illusion that didn't become as real as they desired it to be, now they were betrayed and ripped off by this malicious act.

So what, so she'd crapped out? Plowed through a pile of cash, she'd done it before, money was for spending, life for living, but when some people, maybe a working class wage slave without the meaning of fire, had the audacity to judge, right down the bridge of some fattened nose, or perceivably take a certain joy in their notion of her failure, it infuriated Piper. There were always going to be those that liked all her pretty songs, loved to sing along, but would never know what it means.

When Piper finally let her words rest, she and Robert shared a smirk, and a mentally saturated Claire retreated to her notes.

The next question came, and Claire's voice resonated with an aroused respect. Clearly she was convinced that Piper's reputation as a verbal cannon was well earned. She also realized that under the civil mask of Piper's linguistic discourse hovered the real threat, that she just might pitch Claire out that floor length picture-window.

"You were the front girl for Diary, why aren't you singing in your latest project?"

"Hey, we were a good punk band, and what I did was fine for that. But with The Wild, I get to concentrate on playing guitar, and I leave the singing to someone who can really sing."

"Is that your younger brother Buck?"

Leaning forward, she placed an elbow on the table and lowered her full framed glasses. Piper's sharp green eyes could look right into a person with a naked honesty that captivated attention and demanded truth. The force of her stare gave Claire a quiver.

"You heard our demo, what do you think?"

The interviewer is not to become the interviewed, Claire knew that cardinal rule from college. So, she sipped from her coffee, Robert lit another smoke, and Piper waited. After a quiet consideration, Claire met those verdant eyes. "Piper . . . I burnt a copy."

With a voice of silky tones, Piper reclined back with her ice-water.

"Glad you like it."

7

What was his favorite time of morning was now Everett's favorite time of evening.

Del came from around the end of the bar with a faint smile, and pointed to his watch. Out of the deep fog built from a full day of drink, Everett strained his eyes across the room, squinting to interpret. It took him a long bobbing moment to process Del's gesture, and when the meaning of the request hit him, he replied with a secret wink.

It struck Del humorous, in his sobriety, that the gesture had been but one of many padded reminders to think about leaving. Everett took it as a sign to make more time with April. Pathetically funny.

Whatever, that was fine with Del. As long as Everett knew to call it a day soon. The evening shift bartender was about to come on and had no patience for the likes of April and him.

Hanging on each other and swerving in and out of a staggering walk, they were a spectacle. Emerging from the front door of the lounge, together they sang a drunken medley of hits they shared a mutual familiarity with. Staying not too long in one tune, they slipped from melody to melody, blending lyrics and phrases from a battery of old songs.

April weaved to a stop, scanning the parking lot, and leaning on Everett. In a second she lost the music, immediately disoriented, distraught, searching for her car with a thick desperation. But on spotting the boat-like auto, emotion whirled back another one-eighty and she pointed with an exclamation.

"Over there!"

That kicked their medley off again, into the first verse of the old army song. Three lines of that quickly degenerated into about a half-stanza of a show tune, and that morphed into some pop song. By the time April stopped in front of her driver's door, they'd sampled a handful of others, and were now finishing the chorus theme of an old television show.

Digging in her purse for keys, she was slowed by a burst of drunken laughter. Shoving her purse into Everett's hands, she began pawing through it with sudden and violent purpose. Standing there with a slight waver, Everett found the words to an old country song, and while still holding the purse open, gave it a sing.

His soft serenade ended quickly when she threw her arms up into the air, grasping a large round key-chain.

"The keys, the keys!"

Holding them up and jangling them in joy, she shouted again.

"I have the keys!"

Unlocking the door and climbing in the car with sprawling difficulty, April rolled down the window. Everett handed her purse off, and then he leaned down closer to collect an impulsive sloppy kiss. Propped against the car to steady himself, he lit a smoke and dropped his head, doing his best James Dean.

"You want to follow me?"

She burst into another cackle, reached up, grabbed his face in her hands, and kissed him again.

"All the way to hell."

The quick fiery response made him smile. He took her lips again. When they broke for air, she fired up her old land yacht with a prolonged whine and a great rattling roar.

He sauntered in front of her car on the way to his ride, knocking a rhythm on her hood. She revved her engine in response and the yacht let out a pained rumble. By the time Everett was seated in his car, he looked up to see April driving behind him and flashing her brights playfully.

Starting the Cadillac, he prepared to back out. But the yacht was closer to him, abruptly. There was no room to leave.

Annoyed, he craned his head over the back seat, and she waved deliberately. It was the silly earnest expression on her face that made him laugh. He waved back, both to respond in kind, and to get her to back up.

When she understood his intent, she threw it into reverse. The boat lunged backward. With her wheels at an angle, she smashed into a car parked behind her.

The impact startled and scared her, she panicked. Everett could see the distressed confusion on her face as she jabbed the yacht into gear and quickly sped past him. He moved to follow, but stopped when blinding headlights leapt from the darkness, followed by a flood of colored light and the sharp blast of a shrill siren.

A police car had been idling in the dark, in front of the small strip-mall adjacent to Diamond Jack's. The officer had witnessed the spectacle of Everett and April, including the smash resulting from her impaired driving skills. He sped past April's car and blocked her path with his vehicle.

The officer topped off his dark blue uniform with a rigid flat-brimmed hat and stood behind the protection of his driver's door. Leaving his lights flashing, he shined his powerful spot, illuminating the yacht and highlighting April's shocked and anxiety-twisted expression. She began to claw desperately through her purse searching for a way out.

On observing the frantic action of April's movements, he called for backup, and then stealthily approached the automobile, a hand on his sidearm. She sluggishly reached for the window crank. It took a long series of rolls for April to get it halfway down, gaining several inches with each attempt, and when her hand came out of the car to help push the top part of the slowly rolling window down into the door, the officer gave a shout.

"Don't move!"

April couldn't move a muscle, the effects of the liquor were nothing compared to the paralysis of fear his voice instilled. She just sat, waiting to be collected by the long arm of the law. The officer's voice calmed to that of a stern parent as he apprehended April without incident, moving her from the yacht, to the bright flashes of his police car.

Placing her against the back door, the officer turned her around, quickly pat searched, and then cuffed her. He left April leaning alone and returned a call on his mobile body radio, pushing a button on his chest to speak some coded response. Strolling back over to the yacht with a long black flashlight, he began scanning its contents.

From across the parking lot, Everett had seen the scene unfold. He'd watched as the officer opened her door and secured April from her car. Shutting down his ride, he got out and slammed the door behind him.

Overtly drunk and pissed off as he approached the officer, he made an effort to mask his anger with a chummy tactic at first.

"Officer, what seems to be the trouble here?"

The officer was slightly startled and turned sharply to dispatch Everett.

"Sir, I am in the process of dealing with this individual, may I ask you to step over there, please?"

The officer politely, in an official, almost mechanical manner gestured for Everett to move out of the way.

"Hey, Officer Friendly, nobody's looking for anyone to get tough here, right?"

"Sir, I suggest you leave the area."

"You. Telling me . . . what to do?"

"Sir, you appear to be intoxicated, please clear the area."

Right then it dawned on the officer just who he was talking to; this was Everett Wild, notorious drunk and disorderly.

"Sir, this is your last warning to clear the area."

Another two police cars pulled onto the scene, two more officers got out from each car. Everett barked loudly.

"Oh, here comes the cavalry, you boys here to help arrest this dangerous lady? Thank the heavens there's four of you. Did you bring the dogs?"

April swallowed hard, repressing a swell of nausea, and decided to get back into her car. Attempting to do so, she was immediately stopped by the officer, who was becoming increasingly agitated. He snatched her by the arm as the other officers approached the scene.

"Ma'am, I'm going to have to put you under arrest for driving a vehicle under the influence."

The first officer passed her off to the arriving patrolmen. Those officers read her rights aloud, and escorted her to a car. This infuriated Everett, and he exploded in a barrage of abusive verbiage.

"Oh, there is a big man. Hey, big tough man picking on a woman, they pick on you on the playground? Little punk grows up strong and tough with a big bright badge—is that what it is, officer?"

The officer began to walk to Everett, two of the patrolmen close on his heels. Everett physically retreated toward his car, but kept his mouth moving. He reached the Cadillac still barking, and they'd caught up, but now he'd become amused with the attention, the chase, with abusing them.

"Are you here to prove it, prove how tough you all are?" He spoke softly and his words dripped with a venom-laced cynicism.

"Brainwashed little bitches."

These were spiked words, designed to provoke and taunt. "How 'bout one of you at a time, punks? Maybe without the firearms, huh?"

This wild rhetoric tickled the main officer, and he let out a sigh to cover an exhausted laugh. It stirred the stoic facade that was his face. He now spoke easily, with the tone of an old friend.

"Everett, please, if you don't calm down you will force me to take action."

He got real calm, real fast, like someone threw a switch. Everett's posture changed from attack to that of relaxed peace, his shoulders dropped, and he stood on the back of his heels. Smiling broadly, he pulled a cigarette from the pack in his pocket, placed it in his mouth, and spoke with a drunken drawl.

"Tell me what it is."

"Sir, I don't believe you should drive."

Raising his hand with the keys, he displayed them to the officer. He opened the driver's door, locked it, threw the keys inside, and then slammed the door shut, a quick violent ripple in his new calm.

"Right, well, you know what's best, don't you?"

The officer and Everett walked in tandem toward the side of the restaurant. The other two uniforms responded to the officer's wave of dismissal. They retreated to their respective vehicles, packing up April and the rest of the show.

"You just got cut a break, Everett, better make it on home."

Everett had reached the front of Diamond Jack's and started to walk into his sanctuary. The officer's hand gently landed on his shoulder and he carefully steered Everett away from the door. His tone was confidential and invested with real care, his shift had ended fifteen minutes ago.

"They don't need you in there right now, Everett." Removing the uniform's rigid flat-brimmed hat, he revealed his rounded mid-thirties face; a soft earnest expression was framed by a full head of dark curly hair. He escorted Everett over to a pay-phone, mounted into the brick wall of the building. Taking one step back, he examined Everett with some intent, and urgency now attended his voice.

"Why don't you call somebody, come take you home? Anyone? Do you want me to call you a cab?"

Sapped from the energy he'd lost to his anger, Everett really needed another drink, or maybe just to crash. The dark blue official figure of the officer was a reminder to stay wary, but without his hat, the face had captivated Everett enough to relax his guard some. The officer propped him against the wall and asked directly.

"You got a hide-a-key under your bumper or something, key to that car? Everett, do you?"

Shaking his head slightly, a morose wave flooded Everett's face, and from a great distance he told the officer.

"I don't want to drive right now, don't want to."

The timbre of the answer disturbed the officer. He dealt daily with the colorful spectrum of humanity, and always kept professional distance in tone and manner, nothing but the facts. But the fact here was he knew Everett, or at least who he had been.

Five years ago he'd broke up a brawl at this very bar, and while running names during the arrest one name jumped out at him. The officer had heard he'd lived around here from another cop, who had recounted a domestic disturbance call, including some reported shotgun blasts directed toward noisy geese at the Wild residence. Some domestic call shooting off a shotgun wasn't too big a surprise for an FW cop, but the officer realized that this disturbance was Everett Wild, the Everett Wild, songwriter.

A country music fanatic, the officer was into old songs, not this light-in-the-pants pop they pawn off today. He admired any melody with quality, but really loved the spirit of the outlaw country movement. There he had found tunes with depth, meaning, and rhythm that touched the quick of his being.

The man stumbling before him had written such songs. One cut in particular had hit, and crossed over. 'Touch of Grace' was one of those tunes so ingrained into country, oldies, and classic rock stations, that it would play daily forever, until the end of radio itself.

It was crazy, here was a man who had lived with the legends, the giants, this officer's heroes, and now he could barely stand, but for the brick of the wall behind him. Made the officer sick and sad at heart to see what a life of liquor can do to someone. Even pitifully loaded, Everett's appearance and energy told him he was no ordinary man, and the officer had to question why someone so sharp would dull himself to this.

"Look, Mr. Wild, promise me you will not drive, you'll leave here, call someone, get some food, go home, sleep it off, Ok?"

"Yeah, no problem."

Everett's answer came fast and slurred. It was coherent enough for the officer. He wanted nothing but to go home, he hadn't seen his wife or baby daughter in what seemed like a year, and this exchange had turned something inside him, a dull anxiousness now pulled at his stomach.

"Put it in gear, kid."

This dismissal made the officer smile, and it was meant to. He thought to deliver one of the dozen ready-made morality tales that he had at his fingertips, but the fire in Everett's drunken eyes, that devilish sneer, stopped him. What the hell was he going to tell this living embodiment of some outlaw song?

"Take care of yourself, Mr. Wild."

The officer stepped back and donned his rigid flat-brimmed hat, took a last look at the character before him, shook his head in disbelief, and with an exasperated chuckle, headed for home.

Leaning against the brick, Everett followed the path of the wall to the corner of the building, and then to the back of the restaurant. Beside the dumpster, hidden in shadow from the dim flood of the back-porch light, he let himself crumple into a pile. Spinning, spinning, spun, he relaxed into his nausea, disappearing into sleep.

8

A shrill pick-scratch tore from her guitar and resonated like a scream.

The plush room ended a long narrow hall. It was the signature space in an upper-end studio on the edge of Belltown. Two overstuffed Italian black leather couches, several matching chairs, and fabric-covered acoustic foam lined the walls.

Before a large window, a massive mixing board of switches, dials, and bright little lights peered into a recording booth, where there was a large padded microphone, and more acoustic foam. Piper kicked a stool out from under her as she stood abruptly. She shredded into her lead, her mouth moving with the sounds she played.

Her head jerked just perceptibly as she anticipated the playback. The tassels of her jacket, the fray of her denim, her hair, everything she was moved with the rhythm. She gave it all away, playing from the heart of her struggle.

Letting her feedback choke to a screeching finish, Piper brought the song to rest. With a fresh charge, that certain satisfaction only the music could give her, she placed her

Gretch on its stand. Sitting down on the oversized couch next to Buck she was immediately smothered in a hug.

"What do you think?"

Buzz, the production engineer, always bellowed.

"Think what?"

Behind the big board, he was already hitting playback and her solo was heard again. Starting to mix the guitar with the rest of the band, he feathered dials and shifted his eyes toward the speakers to decipher the next turn to be dialed.

When the playback finished, a frenetic Buck jumped from the bench with Piper in his arms and twirled her around.

Setting her down, he started dancing stutter-step in a circle, on the warpath, calling up the ancestors, yelping out that sound, one hand beating against his mouth. Piper and Buzz cracked up, and she gave the big man a loud kiss on the top of the head.

Piper and Buzz knew each other from the early days. Her habits, interests, attitudes and priorities would never integrate Piper within the framework of the social mainstream. She'd never held so much as a part-time job, not ever, let alone full-time, punch-clock and lunch-break type gainful employment.

There would be times when she made some money, good money from her music. But many more times, especially at the beginning, she did not. From the start, her friend Buzz had been there to facilitate her in a part-time profession.

Buzz, or Ernie as his mother had named him, was a large man who dressed and self-identified himself as a biker, though he had no official affiliations. Barrel-chested with huge tattooed arms and bright blue blood-stoned eyes, Buzz's deeply etched crows-feet mapped out his forty-some years. He'd moved to Seattle from Northern California with a brand new plan, he was going to grow a lot of pot, and make a lot of money; his plan worked.

From the moment his van full of equipment pulled into town, Buzz was rolling. By the time the Seattle sound started to explode, he lived in a nice condo on Queen Anne, owned several clubs, an indie record label, and twelve different houses in three different counties, pumping out tons of grass, six houses harvesting one month and six the next, on rotation.

A huge percentage of the population in the Northwest smoke pot; the young, old, rich, poor, health-nuts and derelicts, business owners, techno-nerds, fags, skaters and slackers, suits and ties, and especially the blue collared working guys, they all love grass. Buzz, and people just like him, financed directly by marijuana prohibition, provided the setting, the buildings, facilities, stages and fuel, from whence the seeds of an individual and unique scene were able take root and eventually blossom. Early on, it was weed that paid all the bills.

Buzz loved to have PartyGirl play. He'd set up all-age shows, taking a big loss at the bar, just to accommodate quality. He cleaned all kinds of cash in the clubs, ticket and beverage sales, numbers at the door, reported revenues, all assortments of money games.

Knowing Buzz meant Piper could gig at will, and still make ample side money on her own time and terms. From the moment she got her car keys, she would house-tend, plant-care, watering, clipping, and manicuring. Sometimes she'd mule pounds around and deal some, but she didn't put her name on anything.

Piper became Buzz's right-hand gal for years, his main troubleshooter, watching over a string of his houses and filling in for any pinch. Buzz insisted the plants always responded positively to women, and that may be so. In any case Piper had the natural knack, a so-called green thumb.

But the bigger reality, the reason she was so good, was that she approached growing with the same finesse and artistic precision that she did her music. That artistic bent for detail and specificity, the patience to let something take root, the consistence of care it takes to induce a flowering, nature and nurture, it all translated from her music to her growing. The work taught her a greater understanding of living things.

Piper was intimately exposed to, and instructed in the intricate science of indoor growing, and her life became intertwined with the culture of the outlaw. It wasn't good enough for Buzz to have someone tend his crop and make all kinds of cash. He was an avid fundamentalist in his belief that hemp, used as food, fuel, medicine, and much more could save the planet, and demanded that once one knew the secrets, was instructed in the art, they were clergy, tenders of a sacred flame.

Piper was raised without religion and hadn't attended any school past the seventh grade. It was from an eclectic experience that she forged her own world view. Believing she was on the right side of an unjust war, she decided that not to grow cannabis was to commit a sin, an outright act of cowardice, a convenient rational that left her free to operate.

Shut your mouth about the business, locations, numbers, names, people, places, and faces. It's that easy. When in doubt, ask for an attorney.

Anything you say can and will, can and will, be used against you, against you, against. Not everybody is a cop, but you never know who might be, so every facet of her life became secret squirrel. Code names, cloak and dagger, watch to see if you're being watched, never drive directly anywhere, give an exact time for a meet, or meet anyone new.

Some could sense, subconsciously even, that she was not playing by the rules. All her time to do whatever. All that music equipment.

Whether she'd written some rock and roll, or grown some high-grade grass, there was a demand for explanation, to know how she lived. Where she got her cash. Why did she get to be so free?

Why her?

The real answer was because she was a doer, she did things, took risks, empowered herself. She believed you take a chance while you still have the choice. Everything she ever had was earned, any inference of something else and she felt offended.

Who was anybody to say different? On what grounds? She saw all the concerned questions boiling down to really just one.

Where was their share?

Suspicion and measured civility marked a discourse with Piper if you didn't know her. Always ready for the aim of any inquiry to invade, evaluate, to attempt a calibration of some comfortable social norm she wasn't adhering to. She thought anyone who feels they are not free must yearn to wing those that are, and so many of the miserable would lust to break her spirit, and if they only knew, bust the operations.

She knew most people didn't even have a problem with grass, not really, seemed invariably they smoked themselves. Of course, given the chance some loved to preach and sermon on about saving the children from dangerous drugs and desperate criminals, but that wasn't true either, that's not what anybody was mad at. Piper figured it was all envy, envy and fear, of her, or any manifest example of freedom and independence.

In Piper's mind the only real Americans left grew hemp, period, but if asked, she always had a cover story for any inquiry.

"I play in a band, and do night-time janitorial work to make a little cash."

Only Buzz or Piper worked at the Office, the main mother house, a very nice brick two story home in a middle class suburb with a sound view.

Buck could clearly remember the day his older sister brought him by the Office. She loathed the endless low-end daycare Everett brought Buck up on. Just old enough to concretely form that opinion, not old enough to do much about it, she spent all the time she could with her young brother, who, at six was still small for his age.

It was just before three and Piper had to go by the Office, she'd never brought Buck to work before, but figured at the time he was just young enough to not notice anything weird about stopping to feed her friend's cat for an hour or so. She left Buck in front of the television on the main floor. They weren't going to be there long, she needed to get a few important things done, some chores upstairs, a quick check on the work in the basement, then they were going to catch a children's animation festival downtown.

When she came downstairs to see the TV entertaining an empty room, and saw that the door to the basement was ajar, the light of heaven escaping out the crack, she was hit with a wave of guilt, fear, and panic. But there Buck was. Standing at the bottom of the old wooden stair, his features in shadow, his figure silhouetted by the brilliant halide.

Piper walked down the stairs and simply put her arm around his shoulder. The two stood beholding the crop. Buck's expression was transfixed in a state of stunned wonder.

"Pretty cool, huh, Buck?"

Her question broke the silence and Buck's focus. Slowly he panned his head to meet her smile. Suddenly he broke into an attack, an ecstatic shock. His little face twisted with an impish glare and he laughed so hard as to hurt his sides, impede his breath, and produce tears.

Past an initial concern, and then a discomfort, his continued laughter became infectious. Piper's smile broke into a chuckle, and soon she burst out with a storm of mirth. Perhaps when they played music they could create an inseparable vision, an interaction so real as to heal, that came close to the grace of that moment, the afternoon they stood together in the basement, surrounded by contraband, attended to by a chorus of crazed laughter.

The truth was told, and it was apparent that the emperor wore no clothes; every hip kid from the lower classes of Federal Way knew that it was something to be when one grew up, a grower. The politics of contraband, the reality of the underground, the art and science of the indoor, it all came in turn to influence her view of society, coloring her relationship to popular culture, to the mainstream. The impetus of her music was still rooted in her own need to rock, but she began to see her music as a place from which to speak, her voice.

Music first, was the line she drew in regard to work, no ongoing responsibility that couldn't be walked away from today, right now. It was an innate knack she'd always had, knowing just how much to take, how late to stay out, and how close to get in.

A sensibility that she employed in all aspects of her life, this intuition, and a dedicated discipline to follow it, continually saved her ass.

It was shortly after four o'clock as Buck and Piper stepped out onto the front porch, witnessing a large green sport utility vehicle drive slowly by the end of the long driveway. Twice. On the second sighting, she knew.

They were coming. Next second they'd be everywhere, a bunch of them. The jack-booted thugs were marching in a military beeline toward the house.

Each of them had one hand on the shoulder of the soldier in front, all were armed to the teeth with assault weapons and sidearms. Decked out in matching black battle outfits, they wore riot helmets with face visors, obscuring their features. The one in front hid behind a body-length bulletproof clear shield.

They all trotted in a row behind the point-man, in back of them followed a slow moving parade of vehicles. The house was becoming surrounded and they shouted threats and instructions through a megaphone. Piper calmly shut the front door.

An electric shot ran over her body. Before she knew it, she was down the basement stairs, pulling all the starts out by the roots with one arm, holding Buck with the other. Then she grasped at a plant and ripped it up by the roots, tossing it on its bucket, pissed and distraught at the futility of not being able to do one darn thing.

A jarring pounding above seized hold of them, and she tasted the acid of her stomach. Taking a deep breath, she put Buck on his feet and the two brushed by the tattered American flag tacked to the base of the stairway, and began the long slow hike upstairs. Shutting the basement door behind them, she paced the three strides to the fridge, and with Buck behind her, they turned to greet their assailants.

The bacon had piled itself in the kitchen. They appeared to her as a macabre set of keystone cops. Framing the doorway with faces and stances so exaggerated as to startle, they were drawn like a cartoon, animated to the point of parody, amusing but for the sick gravity of righteousness, a willingness to commit any violence in the name of their law.

Some appeared at the two windows, sticking halfway into the kitchen, poking in their helmeted heads and pointing their arsenal of handguns and rifles. There was a frantic chorus of their screams and shouts. Piper cautiously raised her hands, still shielding Buck.

This act of submission was done in slow defiance. Claiming at least the pace of the events unfolding, she eased down to her stomach. Buck at her side, they met the guns without a flinch, keeping a cold visual contact, until a black boot came down on her neck and Buck was swept away.

"Move and you're dead."

It's one of those lines every uniformed punk wants to
lay claim to. The reason this guy got up in the morning. A
mid-sized assailant, he ran from one uniform to the other
exclaiming how he had almost shot Piper, how close he'd been,
that close, to pulling that trigger, so close, how high he was on
adrenaline, how well they'd all done, and again and again, how
lucky she was that he hadn't shot her.

Teams scoured the house with their regimented swat-
trained tactics. Courageously, they took out the bathroom and
bedroom doors, kicked open all the closets. In the big climactic
sequence, they gathered around the basement door and
communicating with the jerking, pointing, and gestures of a
fattened first-base coach, they bashed in the final door, starting
down the stairs.

Piper could feel their stomping vibrate through the
floor into her cheek, and she struggled to get a good breath
as the boot at her neck tightened down. She'd love to break
this punk, Piper could probably do it in most circumstances.
Had to remember this was all business, grocery clerks here to
collect a bill, her temper would do no service here, she had to
stay calm.

Buck was clutching an officer-issued teddy bear. Barely
holding back tears as several armed guards led him into the
front room, he was plopped on the couch. From across the
hall, Piper stole a wink as to say, don't worry 'bout a thing little
brother, this is holy ground.

With just that look, the strength of her gaze, Piper
provided the reassurance, the cool, Buck needed. The tears
dried and he dropped the bear to the ground, struggling to
move closer to his sister; the kid was alright. Piper would
always remember just how tough that little guy was in that
moment, it furnished her a further resolve to stay calm, to get
through this ordeal without anyone getting hurt.

It was the next thing that really pissed her off, a phrase
each of them would remember forever, especially young Buck.
It was a shout from one soldier to the others as they braved
their way downstairs, a panic about not being to see around
the flag, tacked up at the bottom. The command came in the
form a frantic shout.

"Tear it down, tear down the flag!"

The words echoed in the minds of Buck and Piper
forever; tear it down. This bunch of tough guys, these were
not Americans, these are not men, no real crime had been
committed, there was no victim here, save the truth. Grass
roots capitalism, it was all done by the boot straps, something
had been made here from nothing, from seed to sea of green.

And here came those that wanted their cut.

The fashion of the day would rather have them hooked
on vicious drugs with designer names and ad campaigns,
to have no recognition of marijuana as an ancient herbal
alternative. Many friends of both Buck and Piper were
already addicted to an alarming spectrum of brand new and
experimental pharmaceuticals, doctor prescribed and served at
school.

Where's the revenue if someone can just grow some
grass? So when they come, it's in a swarm. Hard to say how
many more showed after the original bust, they seemed to just
keep coming. Piper was arrested and taken away, Buck was put
into custody, and it took a week of red tape for Everett to get
him back.

Indelibly marred with the sight of the police cuffing
his sister, Buck would never trust a uniform in his life. He'd
witnessed too much, too early, and no amount of officer
friendly would ever again regain his trust, or instill any belief
in good government bull. The experience of the bust was a
memory burnt into his mind, images and events he would
never be able to avoid, never forget.

Buzz bailed out a long list of others, but Piper was released due to her clean record, and when prosecution came they filed against Buzz and most of his associates. Piper was not charged with anything and the issue of Buck wasn't mentioned at all. There was a standard policy in place at the time to avoid any litigation involving minors.

Up at Whistler Mountain skiing when the whole deal went down, Buzz came home to paperwork indicting him of criminal charges, but never quit growing, not for one day, tending crops between court dates, and even most of his associates were put back to task. Piper counted her lucky stars and swore off that kind of work, remaining poor, yet free and unafraid, until Diary signed its first deal and she saw some publishing money.

So she understood when she learned Bones was moving pounds of Canadian grass all over the southend. An inspired bass player, and sociable guy, he was never late to practice and seemed like a streetwise enough kid. She'd known him forever, her brother's little friend who turned out so tall, never had he messed with guns or needles, grass was his business, his risk.

Any list of suspected growers had Piper on it, all kinds of flags came up every time someone ran her name. She had a brother, that was nothing but a click of a button. They build profiles, legal or not; she'd witnessed how cops trailed, tapped, and tracked Buzz, how they broke the law more than he did.

She'd learned paranoia doesn't mean anything when there are armed men hunting anyone who inhales. How true that was struck her when she traveled to Amsterdam. A grower went to A-dam in the nineties like a poet to Paris, generations before.

Well aware that weed, the way of any prohibitionist, can become an all-inclusive way of life, she worried about her younger brother. Growing was arguably the right thing to do, but what's illegal can land one in trouble. Piper couldn't stand the thought of her brother being in a cage, and if she had a legacy to lend, she'd rather it be on a stage, or in the studio.

Buck had a part-time job working with children that made him some money. He was way too much of a socialite to grow, and he seemed content for now to have free reign at Bones's stash. But the lure of easy money has a very strong appeal.

Piper swore she wouldn't leave him to learn on his own, not again, not like when he was young. She was here to manifest a reality. She wanted Buck to understand that his true potential, his future, would come from the call of their music, from The Wild.

With scaled-down activities these days, Buzz now kept himself well insulated from any hands-on participation; he owned, answered questions, made connections, and collected a healthy monthly stipend, but considered himself in retirement. With a large chunk of laundered cash he had built this studio. He took his time and learned how to mix and record, and gave ridiculously good deals to friends and anyone he liked, or thought he could learn from.

This was the first time Buck had recorded in a studio, in any environment outside a garage, or some live tracks at a show. The microphone, these headphones, it seemed forced and set up to him. It messed with his melody.

In the recording booth it was take four, and Buck began muttering. With a deep breath, he checked himself, let go, and sang. After a verse, he was technically fine, but he felt uncomfortable and agitated, and stopped again.

Piper's voice came over the intercom from the control booth, sending Buck's body into a perceptible slump.

"What's up?"

Ignoring the question, Buck paced, it was hard to swallow and he wanted to cry. Great, he thought, get here, all the way here, and then be somewhere else. Be here, be here now, he told himself over and over again.

His mutter became a rhythmic chant, and the pace of his pacing increased as he kept his face to the ground, avoiding looking up to the window where Piper sat with Buzz. She must know. He could do better.

What was wrong with him? If he didn't do what he could do right now, what was he doing? Was he living up to her investment in him?

His voice felt fine. He felt fine, but he wasn't connecting to, well, to anything. It was all lonely, detached, way out, like he was singing into some void.

"Buck, what the hell are you doing?"

The question cut at him and he turned from his pacing and finally met Piper's eyes with a wounded look of frustration. He clutched the sides of his head and suddenly expressed in a long and guttural ear-shattering scream what could never be said in words. The sound set Piper back in her chair and left Buzz scrambling for a volume dial.

"Did we get that?"

Piper's question was immediate, her voice urgent; Buzz nodded in the affirmative and played it back. Buck had landed on the wall of the small room, one foot propped behind him, leaning into the sound-insulating foam in a discouraged pout. When suddenly his own voice leapt back at him from the speakers, and that disturbing, ear-gripping barbaric yelp again filled the studio, it brought him to his feet.

What Piper heard was a defiant expression of a profound struggle. A unique, full, round and resounding scream, a vocal of sound and fury, perfect to start the first song. As soon as the playback finished, she leaned into Buzz's ear and spoke softy.

"We're gonna use that on the first cut."

Making a note, she handed the clipboard to Buzz, took her jacket off and then walked into the booth, grabbing her guitar from its stand and putting on a set of headphones. With a deep and deliberate breath, Buck put his headphones on and then took two steps to stand next to his sister. Stomping on a pedal on the floor, she tuned up, lit a smoke, and produced a sneer. "Let's hit that from the top, Buzz."

As the playback started, Piper began to play with it. She angled herself physically so Buck had a wide breadth of space, but the intensity of her playing was so infectious that he became entranced. Very still, he simply watched her, listening, distant, then, at the top of the verse, he was suddenly very present.

A feel and fluidity filled the studio that was absent previously, and his inertia was summoned from such a place that his voice slid into the air, breaking into song before he'd given himself permission to do so. Buck's movements were slight, smooth, and few. Propelled by his connection with Piper, absorbed in the moment, the words and music, his instrument became free.

It was flawless.

When his voice released the last phrase, and her pick ran the neck of the Gretch, grinding to a close, the song finally rested, and neither could do more than smile.

9

Her fingertips lightly traced the naked curve of his body.

A flickering hue from a few scented candles infused the air with a thick scent of cinnamon and bathed his bare skin in a glow as Skyler slept in serenity. It was so late as about to become early, and the first bright of morning expanded dimly across the cramped and cluttered front room. Piper hadn't slept, she'd been brooding.

She blew out the candles, slipped on some boots, grabbed her jacket, and crept out the door into the drizzling damp of the morning air. A lonely howl from a train on the tide-flats echoed into the slowly stirring city as she splashed her way up McKinley avenue to the small smokebox on the Ave, entered, and ordered some hashbrowns and a large orange juice. It was shortly after six and the small greasy café was already thick with blue collars getting ready for their commute, so she sat at the table to the left of the front door, next to the fan, and stared out the window.

Southeast Tacoma was the last part of 'The City of Destiny' to feel its restoration. The neighborhood's aged homes and buildings, some over a hundred years old, were thick with working class families, the aspiring young investing into a shady part of town, ethnics of every type and legal status. Currently budding into a nicer place than it had been in a long time, it remained a semi-dangerous spot with an eclectic mix of indigenous social trash of all colors.

Perhaps the only smart thing she'd done was cash in her last chip to buy her small rambler, her sanctuary, a tiny dwelling, a remnant from the deposits of military housing that littered the area. Built in the early forties, the small gray home was a single story, with a second bedroom as big as a large closet. It sat on a good sized lot, with a partial view of the sound from the furthest corner of the yard.

She'd bought it for less than half then what it was now worth. It took the last of her cash. Buzz had done some custom work for her, making the inside quite nice.

Piper didn't believe in mistakes. When she was truly honest with herself, she knew a profound part of her demanded real change. If there was anyone she could wake up next to forever, it was Sky.

The drone of the morning's news blared from the suspended television, and blended with the tobacco cackles and grinding hacks emitting from the early rising alcoholics that lined the counter. Piper's hashbrowns were as good as gone the moment they hit the table. After pounding her orange juice, she asked for a second order of browns, and decided a little coffee couldn't kill anybody.

Let's look at this again, a choir of voices agreed in her head. She eased a tattering envelope out of her jacket pocket, and unfolded the paper inside. After reading the words, she could find nothing to console, or explain, no rationale, no excuses that she knew.

Studying the words, absorbing each letter, she read the information repetitively, and it was still the same. She hadn't believed any of the home kits, and had been skeptical when the doctor told her himself, demanding he put it in writing.

With a quick calm, she folded the paper back and returned the envelope to her pocket.

When it rains, it pours.

The warmed mug felt good in her hands and she propped her boots up on the windowsill. Time to think, to mull. She was halfway through her first thought when a drenched silhouette appeared from behind the telephone pole directly outside the widow, next to the newspaper boxes.

She would know his shape anywhere, her smile appeared as suddenly as he did. With his tee-shirt and jeans wet from the walk, his hair matted in clumps and clinging to his brow, Skyler sat down just as the second round of browns came, so Piper scraped half the order onto her plate, presenting him with the rest. He made short work of the potatoes and asked the waitress for some oatmeal.

Scooting his chair around the corner of the table, his hand ran across her back, and he held her far shoulder with a squeeze. Enclosed in his arm, her head curled into his neck and they exchanged a kiss. His hand met hers at the coffee, and each held half as they watched the steam rise from their cup.

Running the side of his face against her hair, Sky breathed in just as deeply as he could. The world slipped away and he ate his oatmeal. They talked about going camping, how each of them loved the mountains, how they planned to hike Rainer together in the spring.

After paying the check it was an easy stroll the five blocks to E street, where they sat down on the bent-up guardrail overlooking the city and sound. Dreaming together, they described their view condo, and a streamside cabin in the woods yet to be built. How they would spend the time of their lives, living at each, together.

They talked about everything, lost in their love for each other. Abandoned totally was the foremost issue on each of their minds. That is, until they got home.

"Piper, I want our kid to grow up living with a Mom and a Dad, together as a real family."

He was playing way past where she was. Talking about getting married, that's what he was talking about, if not, something dangerously close to it. She was still struggling with the idea of what had happened, what to do about it.

"How are you so sure, that's it the right thing, to keep it?" "It?"

He'd answered fully, and shamed her, both, with a word.

"Skyler, The Wild is about to get offered a deal, we are." "Yeah?"

He needed further explanation?

"Are you really with the rest of us? Have you thought about reality at all? About jobs and bills, and all the things parenthood would mean?"

There was nothing, not one thing else on this planet she wanted to do more than play guitar. She'd always been very clear about that. For that aspiration to be compromised to this degree of finality questioned the totality of her own character as she'd always known it.

"It's hard to rock pregnant, Skyler."

What's more it might be easy for the golden son to turn off the tunes, maybe be happy just jamming with some friends, he could do anything, he just happened to play the drums, happened to find her, he hadn't carved a niche out of granite, dreamed his genius in the sweat of his sleep, he never worried about or invested into anything the way she had, he'd skipped the struggle.

In two steps she grabbed her guitar from its stand and flipped a switch, powering a small amp with a large sound. Skyler understood she'd ended the discussion for the present time, and he was as close to pissed off as he was going to allow. The depth and nature of her indecision, and the possibility

of pending action, he knew, could result in the end of their
relationship.

Realizing he'd been encased in his own cocoon of what
he thought life was about to become, Sky ripped his shirt off
and tossed it on the radiator. He understood his propensity to
be impractical, but knew he was as far from stupid as a person
could be. You can have it all, you just have to determine what
the definition of all is, and apparently now they were going to
have to re-define it mutually. "Let's get away for a week."

Piper struck a howlingly dissident chord, and Sky
shouted to be heard over the sustain.

"Go out of town and think."

Crossing to her, he slipped his arms around her waist.
She muted the chord into a low mournful grind. The guitar
gave a low growl and her smile returned when he whispered in
her ear.

"Whatever happens, we'll be together." Her answer left
her lips with a kiss. "Deal."

Skyler released her softly. Then he left to the kitchen. His
fingertips trailed through her hair.

Hers flew to the fret-board, letting her ax rip, not
worrying about the early hour.

10

It was the rattling racket of the garbage truck that woke him.

He'd read about bums dying in a dumpsters, scooped into death because they passed out in a seemingly safe metal box. It wasn't the thought of being dead that forced him up from the ground. Going out in the garbage, like a bum, that was the thought that made him stand.

The day was as cold as it would get, shortly before sunrise, and a thin blanket of frigid wet covered everything. This hadn't happened in a good while, passed out, sleeping on cement, waking up disoriented and still drunk. Everett hurt, so thirsty, so cold.

Grabbing the green metal dumpster with both hands, he was sure he was going be sick. A cold sweat started suddenly, as his face flushed with heat, a good breath became hard to take, and he gagged so hard he could feel it in his feet. It was a tremendous act of self discipline, of endurance and determination, standing, breathing, walking.

Accompanied by the first rays of sunlight, Everett staggered out from behind Diamond Jack's. The parking lot was empty save his locked-up Cadillac, and some small red car parked way in the rear. Landing against the familiar brick wall, he searched himself for change, slipped some quarters into the phone, and let it ring.

Everett lucked out, the band had jammed late into the night after the recording ended. His father's voice sounded small on the line and Buck was wide awake in moments. Buck's Mustang needed work, so Piper's Colt was the only running rig at hand.

"There he is."

Piper was driving, Buck was in the passenger seat, and quickly he jumped into the back. With a short blast on the horn, Piper pulled the car to the side of the road. Everett opened the passenger door and got in.

"Drive."

The thirty minute wait in front of Diamond Jack's had sobered him some and he was actually hungry. He relaxed into the seat and rubbed his aching legs with long deep strokes that warmed his numbed and tingling hands. It felt good to be out of the cold, welcomed back into the world by his two favorite people.

How often did they ride together in a car? When was the last time? The rarity of the occasion gave Everett an idea.

"You guys real busy this morning?"

The Olympic Peninsula possesses far more shades of green than the human eye can see. It's one of those places on the planet that breathes for the rest. The air that morning was so clear that they'd left the windows open and cranked the radio all the way through Tacoma, over the bridge, and up the highway into the most beautiful part of the Northwest.

A few turns and a little while later, they'd been off the main road for miles, and Everett was the only one that knew where they were going, or where they were. A small country store appeared on the edge on the woodland road and Everett pointed to pull over. Piper parked the Colt, collected some cash and foraged into the store as Everett remained in the passenger seat listening to Buck, who leaned way up on the back of the front seat, talking.

"Well, it took me a whole day just to keep me from chewing on the mike."

Everett opted to comment on the condition on the Colt rather than Buck's prattle.

"This thing's a death trap."

"But Buzz said that vocals are usually the hardest part." Finding Piper's smokes in her purse, Everett lit one. "There's technique to all that, Buck, you learn by doing it."

He turned up the radio.

"Take this fella, couldn't even steal a decent song."

Piper returned to the car and opened the door, hotdogs in her hands and a couple of bags pinched in her arms.

"Hotdog for Buck, couple with chili for Dad, one for me." She set hers on the driver's seat and disappeared back into the store for a moment, emerging with two boxes of beer. "Couple half-racks for the boys."

Piper handed Everett the two twelve-packs of beer and he carefully fit them into the space before him on the floor. To make room he put his right leg out the window; resting it on the side mirror. One of his two dogs was already gone.

"Keep the change."

Piper passed the grocery bags back to Buck, who situated the supplies.

"Everything, and a bag of chips."

Grabbing her dog from the seat, Piper started the car, turned the radio station to her liking, and then took a bite. She drove and ate simultaneously. Everett hammered his second dog, cracked a beer, finished it in a chug, and put the empty back in the box.

He opened another and took control of the radio. Tuning it from static to crackling stations, he finally found an old and acceptable melody. He sat back into the small bucket seat, and after a swallow, he offered a beer to Piper.

"Would you believe I'm driving?"

Amused, Everett filled his face with a puzzled look, scratching at his chin.

"When did you get religion?"

The song on the radio ended and there was a station identification complete with a choir singing the call letters in an extended harmony.

"The best oldies of all time, all the time." Everett held a beer up for grabs.

"Buck, bit of the heritage?"

Claiming the beer, Buck leaned forward and turned up the radio. The next song had began to play, 'Touch of Grace.' The intro chords were instantly identified, and Buck, shouting in excitement, hovered in the front seat, slapping Everett on the shoulder.

"Dad, it's your big hit!"

Everett immediately attempted to turn the radio down, as Buck jetted forward and covered the knob with his hand. Everett snatched Buck's hand and bit it, not enough to break skin, but it still sent Buck retreating to the back. Everett reached to change the station and Piper's hand gently stopped his with a touch.

"Come on, please."

He never could say no to her. "Oh, what the hell."

Relenting, he allowed the song to continue at a lower volume. Sitting back, Buck rested his head on his hands and refrained from asking a hundred questions. Be here, right here, right now, listen to the music, just let the song and the wind from the windows fill the car.

It was the kind of song you couldn't help but sing along with. Even Everett was softy humming the chorus when he pointed to a sharp right. Pavement suddenly became a winding dirt road, pounding at the clattering Colt.

A couple miles into the woods the road opened into a partial clearing. They entered a small canyon full of long grass cut into the sea of towering evergreen trees above. Piper circled around the field, and came to rest on the far side under a tree, the car facing the way they came. "I've been here before."

The words left her mouth before she knew she had something to say.

"Yes, you have."

There was a tear somewhere in Everett's voice and he dried it with the rest of his beer.

'Touch of Grace' is one of those songs that doesn't come to a clear cut finish. A soft phrase from the guitar repeats over and over again, gradually fading into the distance. It plays on forever, somewhere, just out of earshot.

"Do you miss it?

"What I miss is your Mother."

Tossing his current empty back into the box, Everett reached forward and turned the radio off before Piper shut the car down. The doors opened and all three walked from the cool shade out into the morning sun of the clearing. The air still had the bite of last night's dew, and the fragrant fresh, which only the mightiest of trees can provide, filled their lungs.

Life was as full as it could be. "Dad, who owns this property?" "You do, Buck, your sister, and me."

Lowering himself one knee, Everett looked in the direction they say heaven is.

"Have you ever seen a sky so beautiful?"

His question floated in the air, as Buck sprawled into the grass, stretched with a twist, and ended up lying on his back. Propping herself against her father, Piper sat down. Everett leaned back, and the three gazed into the jagged lofting clouds decorating the bright blue canopy above.

After a bit, Buck fetched some beer and grabbed his pipe, and a little while after that he went back for the bag of chips and the rest of the warming bottles. Beer could maintain the need for fuel, but didn't take Everett away like the liquor did, the there was no earthly sound his children wanted to hear more in that moment than his voice.

Piper abstained from the alcohol, and didn't smoke any grass, but she continually prompted Everett with bits of her memory and propelled his ramblings. He spun his yarns and told the tales of being on the road, making music, and raising hell. It was rare they were together, and without so much as a sharp word.

The conversation grew, and they listened and laughed at so many subjects under the sun, that the morning passed into late afternoon.

What was a case had burnt down to a few bottles. So they drove to a restaurant overlooking a marina on the edge of Gig Harbor. As Buck was crashed out hard in the backseat, they let him sleep.

Outside their window, boats were coming back in from a day of fun. The last light played on the water as Everett belted down his drink and gestured for the waitress with his empty glass. As hungry as she could be, Piper ordered the halibut and asked for some more ice water.

Seldom were the two alone together, rarer still did they speak of the past. This week Piper had suddenly felt more like an adult than ever and had become filled with questions. She was closely studying the exact kind of hell Everett was living in with an enlightened empathy.

It was easy to see how similar they were. The same sharp mind, a demand for independence, a lack of patience with the world, but she couldn't understand why he didn't move somewhere or do something about his problems. Everett answered back by shutting down, drinking, his memory haunting him to despair.

All that ever made sense to her was action. How many more times would she get this chance? He's semi-sober, a public place, a good mood, so she asked him.

It wasn't a long involved question, she didn't beat around any bush. She just placed her hand over his glass as Everett reached for a drink. Locking into his eyes, she boiled it down to one word, a single syllable. "Why?"

She didn't need to repeat or specify or elaborate, Everett knew the full meaning of her question way past any other words she could have used. He looked at his daughter, this beautiful young woman, a living image of his late wife, and saw there the raw elegance and passion that won his respect and love, and had always taken his breath away. Silence sat with them for a while, and before Everett spoke, he turned his head to stare out the window.

"Before the wreck, and your mother died, before all that, there was a little music money, we were a young beautiful family."

A young beautiful family, the words fell on her like a weight. Buck didn't remember the accident or his mother, to him she was a snapshot of a woman who looked a lot like his older sister. But for Piper and Everett it was yesterday.

"After what happened, with her . . . departed, my music . . . died."

"Music never dies."

"I couldn't find the courage to play, to heal, not anywhere, just gone."

"So?"

"So, I got my straight job, never touched that guitar again, not until I gave it to you."

"So, that's ancient history. I'm asking you, what about now, today and tomorrow?"

The mounting tension was broken by a steaming plate for Piper and another highball for Everett. She dug into her halibut, and he ordered a third. The sting of her concern had left him numb with futility and his feet and hands still had a slight tingle.

What was there to say?

Closing his eyes, he drew a long breath deep into the became dammed at his throat, and he sipped from his drink.

Rubbing the rim of the glass with his finger, he played with the passing thought that he was a man who could not live with himself, but did.

"Piper, I quit music like I should've quit drinking."

Slowly shaking his head at his own purgatory, Everett was struck with a low infectious chuckle. By the time it had slowly boiled into to a laugh, Piper's scowl had been betrayed by her smile. Defiant mirth became a recognition between them, that things were exactly how and what they were, nothing more or less.

Events happen in life and people make choices even out of tragedy, love is eternal and immortal, and that's what it is. The laughter revealed their bond was more powerful than any past, and beyond their present ability to express it. Their pain poured into a roar, and together they howled until the waitress gave them a glare to simmer down.

As they rounded out to the spent side of an exhausted chuckle, Piper's plate was taken away, and Everett paid the check.

11

Everyone has to face the music sometimes.

When Frank said to meet him at the alley, Everett knew he had to make his return. The something somebody had said, about whatever he'd done, some event he couldn't remember, had kept him clear for an easy month. Stopping at the cash machine, he got money to pay for most any average damage he might have created, or at least show that he meant to make good.

Figured he'd meet up with Frank, buy a new ball, have a few belts, and see what was said. He parked in the next lot up, near the scuba store, and walked over, buying a paper out of the box on his way in. The pro shop, directly to the left on entrance, had several new balls on display and he'd stopped to inspect them when he heard Frank's distinctive thundering voice behind him.

"Well, here comes our hero now, folks."

A six-foot five-inch mountain, Frank was a one-time local college football stud who'd played in the Rose Bowl before he blew out his knee and lost his window to the NFL. In three and some decades, he'd become increasingly bloated with the beer, bourbon, and pizza that were his daily diet. Meeting every definition of obesity, his face maintained a flushed fiery glow, and with breath that was ever short, it was easily evident that he was a heart attack about to blow.

Turns out Everett was a true protector, a champion of the alley. There'd been an argument, between the new manager and a couple of obviously wired young punks who'd been told they couldn't have a drink, which turned to a scuffle and then into a brawl. Apparently Everett had cleaned house, and with a grand act of finality sent his bowling ball shattering through the windshield of the wounded and fleeing perpetrators' racy sports car.

Today, the thin balding manager introduced himself as Carl from California, and bought a round of drinks. He then presented Everett with a new ball, and thanked him for pulling those punks off, saying he could bowl all he wanted anytime, no problem, no charge. Details of the event continued to unfold as Frank requested several accounts from each participant and every witness.

Beverly, the bartender, told how the two punks had ganged Carl into a corner and if it hadn't been for Everett, who knows. The cook came out and said he hadn't seen such good action in years. Absolutely giddy, Frank continually demanded of Everett, why he hadn't heard the story before?

All Everett could do was smile and say it wasn't all that.

Some of his snippets of memory began to make sense and layers of anxiety washed away with the first few free drinks as he began to enjoy his hero status. After a while he'd heard enough repetition to feel like he remembered some of the violence and had even kicked in a few appropriate details to the conversation.

Still, there was a nagging tug in the back of his mind, hope he hadn't hurt anyone.

Lunch rush hit pretty quick and the two retired to a booth on the far side of the bar. The regional representative for the company, the only corporate string Everett had on him in the field, Frank had scheduled this meet for some reason. As they sat down, he looked like he was ready to lay it on the line.

After some introductory nervous stammering it became clear to Everett that Frank had called him here to let him go, to offer retirement, to fire him. With numbing ears Everett heard something about a recession, computer programs, customer complaints, new account complacency, and a list of serious accusations regarding inappropriate behavior, including repeated public drunkenness; nothing that fit with the present company image. With the delivery of Frank's memorized message and duty dispensed, silence hit the table.

Bev passed them, and Everett held his empty glass up in gesture for another round. Soon the wound of the news deepened, losing its initial bite, becoming much more sore, but with a little less sting. Sharing a crispness and cadence in their rapport, their speech was a rhythm that had worked for over twenty years.

"So, someone wrote a report, made me the bad guy?"
"Called you a boozer."

"Wait a minute, what? Who?"

"Company officially recommends you get some help.

Look, Everett, the long and the short is, if you walk now you get benefits, your retirement, in consideration to service. They don't want any kind of mess."

"Yeah, so, who said what about boozing?"

Frank tipped the rest of his beer, and swallowed hard. "Some people, mainly . . . Bobby Houser."

The name snapped Everett's expression into a recoil and he almost spit his drink out.

"Houser? What the hell does that punk know about boozing?"

"Well, they appointed him the new guy last month, top dog, and you know what that is." "Politics."

"That's right, that's what it is, Everett."

Finishing his drink with a pound, Everett sat back into perplexed and buzzed confusion, to sort this thing out.

"So, this is how they let you go after all that time. This is it?"

"Same kitty-litter they fed to Blankenship when they canned his fat ass."

"They said all kinds of stuff about Blankenship."

"Well, maybe some of that was true, but Blankenship was a good man."

Everett sat back as Bev arrived with a couple of shots and another pitcher of beer. She caught the tense vibe of the table and left quickly without a word. With a turgid gravity Everett kept his voice very low.

"You goddamn right he was, Frank. Blankenship knew his products, knew his customer, knew how to wine 'em, dine 'em, and sign 'em."

"And that, Everett, is business." "Did you go to his funeral?" "Sent some flowers."

Raising his shot glass in a toast to honor Blankenship, Frank was almost misty. "People loved him."

They each slammed their shot and Everett pushed the glasses to the edge of the table.

"Look, Frank, who is Bobby Houser to tell me what it is?" "Well, you're right, you're so right."

"That little princess. I'm a boozer? Get some help?" "Nowadays it's all MBA's and casual Fridays. Look, I'll talk to Norton, end of the week, see what I can do. I mean getting you full coverage and everything."

Reaching across the table, Frank, who seldom smoked, took a cigarette from Everett's pack. Tapping the butt nervously on the table, he lit a match with some difficulty, and took several deep drags. Bothered by a barrage of thought, he then poured more beer, quenched his thirst, placed the glass carefully before him, and then presented his findings.

"Thing is, they probably want to can my fat ass next."

Racing thoughts ran to verify the validity of Frank's declaration, and after his own quick evaluation, Everett realized it was the truth, his voice an angry and menacing slur.

"So, that's the way they're going to bounce the ball. Huh?" Each man mused his fate.

Reflections of every day of his life that he'd lost to doing and saying things for a company he'd never cared about in the first place came close to drowning Everett, and as this giant wave of waste hit his insides, the only outward response he gave was to finish his highball. He then grabbed a glass and poured beer from the pitcher. With his mind crawling to a blank, his spirit was sickened.

"Well, what's it going to be, Everett?"

There was a second when Frank was sure it was about to be splattered suds and broken glass everywhere. But Everett's eyes closed, and he swallowed the beer whole to extinguish the budding inferno of hate welling up inside him. With a wipe of his mouth, he gestured absently for another round.

12

The careening Cadillac knew every twist of the road.

It was Everett who'd pushed too hard, causing a dangerous swerve and a momentary loss of footing. The wet pavement and hairpin corners of Redondo hill, his personal racing track, had almost proven too much for the fishtailing vehicle's round, worn, tires and his blurred ability to drive. Only blind luck and whirling hands had saved them, a second from destruction.

Still, it was as alive as he'd felt since whenever, being that close to death, and his willful whoop expanded into a possessed holler. With the last of the incline behind, he slowed it down to cruising speed. Loved to ride that road, he'd go out of his way to give it a run; when he was loaded he'd drive across town traffic to get a taste of the adrenaline, the turns.

Once he passed the test, it was easy to wind the way, all on back-roads, home. Avoiding the countless cops that constantly combed for drunks was the real trick. To avoid any legal entanglements.

The left turn that brought him onto his street irritated him. Too much traffic and those countless clone homes that

had eaten the woods, enclosing in on his house. It set him in a
bad mood almost every time.

As he eased up to the mailbox, last stop before turning
in the driveway, all of his escape was stripped away and there
he was, again. Pulling up to a stop he saw Piper's Colt and
Bones's black Chevelle on the far side of the garage. That
was where he told them to park, but the sight hit him as an
insult, and further inflamed his injury, giving wind to his
smoldering hate.

A one-time cabin, the Wild Residence was one of the first
structures in the area. Refurbished into a sharp looking little
home by the time Everett bought it for his family, it sat on a
small lake now fed by drainage and run-off. It was a spot only
truly appreciated by passing geese.

Long since buried behind overgrown brambles, the house
sat on a quarter-acre semi-wooded lot. The dirty brown of the
cracking house paint was aged with rust from the bent metal
gutters. A tattered blue tarp was tacked to a corner of the roof.

Buck's mustang was on blocks. The aged and decaying
detached garage was surrounded by recycling and wood piles,
even the rhododendrons had gone wild. As part of the new
neighborhood, it was all quite obviously out of place.

A respectable working class suburban world had
surrounded the home with an army of cookie-cutter houses,
all of the same bland shape and color. What had been earth
and wood was scalped to dirt with the efficient speed of
the corporate machine, an expensive community was being
created. A conformity farm of yardless large boxes, commuter
caves, overgrown condos devoid of any defining character, built
of sawdust and glue, started at the edge of the property line,
and continued in straight lines, ten feet apart, as far as the eye
could see.

Still, once on the property, the shade and shelter of the
trees created a serene protection. The backside of the house

was run over with evergreen foliage and thickets of blackberry bushes so dense that it seemed to be a slice of forest. The lake was periodically stocked with trout, and one could see them jump for food when it rained.

Carrying a paper, his briefcase, and a grocery bag in one arm, Everett had a cheap twenty-two ounce green bottle of malt beer in the other, and slugged it empty. With a staggering saunter, he passed the huge stack of empty bottles piled against the garage. He added another with a toss, creating a clanging cling as the bottle found its place among the rest.

The rotten wood of the front porch was slick algae and standing water. Catching the front door knob and pulling himself steady, he and his wet feet suffered a serious twist to the hip. Keeping his balance with a persistent pressure on the key, once it found the lock, he opened the door with a groaning creak.

With the door shut, the world was locked behind him. But the blaring riff from a single electric guitar cut the air, followed by the crash of a bass and drums. Then came the sound of feed-back, of Buck testing a mike.

"Test, one-two, t-test."

Within a few moments the music was pushing into a loud and pounding crescendo. It was the full sound of a rock band Everett couldn't avoid. The music floated freely across the neighborhood.

Piper stepped on a pedal and the loud distorted rock slipped into a clean, almost country lithe. The rhythm lightened behind her and she executed a haunting and melodious solo. As she finished, Buck slid in with a soft refrain, singing the chorus over the tail end of her last sustained note, melding into the envelope of relentless rhythm.

"Smile, child, . . ."

His voice had the sweet lilt of an obviously honed instrument.

". . . Prayer for the wild, . . ."

The guitar faded and Piper stepped back as Buck sang the last line of the chorus, softly as a lullaby.

". . . sing me a song, let the smile shine a while." Suddenly Piper slammed a long scratch that hammered them back into the familiar hook. Buck jumped into the air delivering a scream over and beyond the band, creating a transition for the opposing dynamic. The guitar slyly recovered its familiar and distorted tone.

Everett was at attention by the kitchen counter. With automated actions, he pulled a bottle out of a brown liquor-store paper bag. He uncapped and poured a large swath of vodka from the fresh fifth into a tall glass.

To this, he added a single ice cube. He drained the glass with alarming speed. Pouring another, he quickly repeated the action.

The house was mainly one room, with a narrow hallway off the kitchen leading to several small bedrooms. The kitchen, dining, and front rooms were the same area, designated and separated by dingy linoleum and worn green carpet, respectively. The small interior was cluttered with a domestic collection of wares only to be described as junk.

Grabbing a remote, he fired up the TV located in front of the window overlooking the lake. The furniture and decor were worn and outdated, mostly the original pieces he'd bought when they moved in. Everett tossed his paper on a small table next to a chair, and collapsed with an exhausted and inebriated sigh.

Once settled, he lit up a smoke. The relaxation near passed him out, but the fiery sting of the cigarette falling from mouth to chest woke him in a painful start. He put out the cigarette and turned up the television, blurring to see the screen.

The band kicked from a brief silence into another set, and it could be clearly heard in the house, not too pervasive, but unavoidable. Everett actively listened for a moment, then gave a begrudging shrug, a silent sort of regard, or at least recognition of development. The better they were the less he wanted to listen.

Turning up the television volume as loud as it would go, a fishing show, he crossed back to the kitchen for another drink. While there, he took a peek out the window at the irritating source of all that noise. Finishing this drink in a belt, he was suddenly struck with a grating disapproval.

He poured the next several, building to a seethe, his stoned eyes piercing the garage.

The band was in full jam when a weaving Everett peeked his head in the partially open door. They were running through the third song on their list, facing each other in a loose semi-circle. Bones was just left of the drums, tucked into the far right corner, and Piper played with her back to the door.

Only Buck might have seen Everett. But he, like the rest of the band, was so focused in the sound that fire could claim the room, the mountain could blow and guided missiles could find the driveway, he'd never have known it. Certainly they couldn't hear Everett as he began to shout for attention.

After waiting for a moment, not noticed or heard, he yelled again, and then gave it a scream. At the third attempt, he'd entered fully into the room, stood by the door, and pounded his fist on the wall, to no avail. The Wild was just wrapped up in their music, too far gone to notice Everett, or anything that wasn't the song they were playing.

Storming into the kitchen, he set his now empty glass on the counter, grabbed the fifth of vodka, and took a hearty pound, leaving the bottle half-empty. Struck by the spark of deep-set inspiration, he marched with a booze-fueled, pissed off, and determined stride to a closet beside the kitchen door. With a confident and righteous countenance he retrieved his old wood-stock twelve gauge shotgun.

The gun tucked under his arm, he entered the garage. Everett gave what he believed to be a more than ample and appropriate amount of time to be noticed. It was a fully fair warning any caring and civilized people would have recognized.

Shaking his head once in dismay, he leveled the shotgun at one of the large PA speakers. The blast destroyed the speaker and abruptly stopped the band. All whirled around, shocked and gazed as stone statues, frozen in disbelief.

With all the attention of the room, Everett calmly pointed the gun at the next closest pile of gear, Piper's amp stack, and with a smile that could cut glass, shot again. The result was a mass amount of high-pitched feedback, a screeching that broke the shocked spell. A clamor of shouts came from the band, and in a second, Skyler jumped over his kit onto Everett.

Drunker than any drowning jerk on payday, Everett could fight with a powerful penchant for inflicting pain, he needn't be cognitive to do so, violence just took over.

Out of the corner of his eye he'd caught the motion of Skyler's attack and sidestepped. The knuckles, meant for the back of his head, just grazed Everett's ear. In a sharp motion he turned and sent Sky sprawling on the floor with the butt of his gun.

Instantly Piper discarded her guitar. She grabbed the towel kept near her water, and ran to the aid of Skyler. Direct pressure to his forehead proved no impediment to the cascade flowing from his brow, blood soaked the towel.

Sky mumbled inaudibly and Piper fought with fear as he began to lose consciousness. Her only solid thought was, get him to the hospital. She guided his hands to the towel, and instinctively he clutched and pressed on his wound.

Deciding his injury could be life threatening, Piper slowly steadied his shaking, as she regained some composure. Bones had sheltered himself behind his amp, a large glass ashtray in his hand. The only one still stunned was Buck, stuck to the same spot, incapable of movement.

Everett was left a screaming tower of rage.

"Can you hear me now? This loud enough for you? Want to make some noise?"

With one movement, Piper clocked her father with a mike—stand to the face. The heavy metal bottom of the stand left a nasty bruise that began to blacken instantly. His response was a powerful back-hand that sent her crashing into the drum kit, a sight that was too much for Buck and his hands found the first weapon they could grab.

An electric bass is a heavy instrument. They're bigger and longer than a guitar and weigh considerably more. Bones had searched forever for his favorite new Fender Jazz in every store around and on the net, month after month, before driving to Portland to pick it up.

The beautiful mahogany neck snapped on impact, but the body of the Fender connected across the low part of Everett's back, a kidney shot, that sent him to his knees. Buck followed up by smacking Everett with what was left of the guitar neck. Then he jumped on him, swing after swing.

A couple really landed, but even still, it only took a few moves and Everett quickly flipped Buck, delivering a swift punch, and then another, before standing to kick him. Bones took the opportunity to ease behind them, helping get Sky to his feet and outside.

Buck curled into a protective ball. Everett only kicked him twice. But he continued to yell and threaten.

Ruining the room in a rampage, he was breaking, smashing, ripping everything he could get his hands on. The starting rumble of Bones's engine stopped him. He bolted out the door with a loud slam as Buck clumsily clamored to his feet.

With the injured Skyler in the passenger seat, there
was no time for Piper to squeeze into the back, and when she
screamed for him to go, Bones punched it. Everett made an
attempt to stop them, bouncing off the hood as the Chevy spit
gravel and tore out of the driveway, peeling away to pavement
and the emergency ward. Gaining his feet in seconds, the
impact of the vehicle threw Everett into a brief fit of pain,
grabbing at his knee with a sick howl.

Madder than conventional wisdom would assume
someone could get, Everett pivoted to run at Piper, who took
off for her Colt. The left leg was dead weight and by the time
he struggled up to her, she was attempting to turn the car over.
Pumping the gas pedal, the engine was slow to fire.

As Everett reached the front of the car, she quickly
locked her door. Slamming his fist on the hood, she jumped
back startled, and he stood in front, as an obstacle. Finally,
with a great grinding whine, the Colt turned over, producing a
large plume of smoke.

Piper revved the engine and threw it in reverse, starting
to back out before it died. She re-started, grinding the gears
into reverse. Again she began to move, but Everett now tapped
on the window.

"Time to listen up."

She backed around, getting in position to pull forward
out of the driveway, to the street. Everett continued to tap on
the driver's window. He was now very calm.

"You are going listen, aren't you?"

Piper flipped her father off through the window.
Before she could move, he bashed that window with his fist,
shattering the glass into a spiderweb. Shocked, Piper threw her
hands up to protect herself.

The Colt jerked to a stop. Everett punched in and pulled
the keys from the ignition, shutting the car off. He then tossed
them into the bushes.

Opening the door, he grabbed a handful of Piper's hair.

By the back of the head, he pulled her out of the car, to her feet. His left leg still trailed behind, but he'd found the march of the righteous, and strode to the house with her resisting in a flail until the roots of her hair were about to give out.

"You crazy bastard, let me go!"

Everett and Piper were en route to the front door when Buck appeared from out of the garage. His shirt pressed to the side of his head, a trickle of blood ran down his collarbone to his naked chest. Everett abruptly greeted him with a stout push toward the house.

"We're having a quiet family night tonight."

The perverse comment rose a chuckle only out of Everett, as he corralled them into the house. Once inside, Piper and Buck made a wide berth as Everett walked in silence across the kitchen to retrieve a tall-boy beer from the fridge. Opening the can with a crack, he slammed the door behind him, and disappeared into the detached garage.

Seconds later, he was in the driveway, carrying his shotgun, casually drinking his beer and loading. Transfixed out the kitchen window, Piper and Buck watched the formal movements of an executioner. Everett walked up to the Colt and pumped two shots into her front tires.

"The bastard shot my car."

Neither of them moved. They were captivated by Everett as he finished the rest of the beer and tossed the can. There was a tremble in Buck's voice as Everett got closer.

"Why aren't the cops here, should we call cops?" Piper stood frozen.

"And piss him off? Neighbors probably think he's shooting at the geese again . . . or they don't care."

"What are we going do?"

There was only one thing to do, and Piper moved from the window with a jerk.

"We're leaving."

"He'll be on us in a second."

The truth of the statement stopped her, she didn't want any more violence, she needed to get to Skyler. A stubborn recognition of responsibility came to Buck, to be a man, to stand up. A real part of him also thought he could reason with the drunk, calm him.

"I can talk to him." "You're crazy." "Go."

Sky was hurt, she had to leave. "Get out of here . . . get!"

She shortly realized she had to get to a doctor herself, now. Everett's violence would pinpoint her as the preferable target. In her current condition, there could be no further risk.

She kissed her brother's cheek, then made her escape down the hallway into her old room, and out the window. Buck felt his wet brow. The cut was superficial, he'd begun to clot, and the blood had slowed to a trickle.

Opening the door sharply, Everett gave the room a winded once-over from the doorway as he rubbed his blackened jaw. He returned the shotgun to its closet. Buck glared at him without a waver, and pointed to his own bloody skin.

"Look what you've done, Everett." The phrase paused Everett. Suddenly he hadn't the courage to look, and went to the fridge for another beer. The composure and quiet tone he assumed was his only pad from the now-crawling realization of his most recent actions.

"Where's you sister?"

Pointing in the direction of the back rooms, Buck kept a stone eye at Everett, his fist clenched. Everett cracked his beer and leaned against the counter. Then with a quick bolt, he rushed the hall.

Buck pivoted to the movement with a wince. After pounding open Piper's old door, near breaking it off the hinges, Everett re-entered the front room. His body in a slump, his expression soaked with a defeated surprise.

"She's jumped out her window."

His hands shook with frustration. He was faced by his own insane behavior. His voice became very small.

"Where?"

"She's gone, you shot her car."

Everett's insides ran wild and instantly his emotions were naked, his answer a muted cry.

"I'm . . . sorry."

Chin up in defiance, he assumed a classic drunken desperation to make things right, marching toward the front door.

"I'll just track her down." "Think you should drive?"

"Think you should open your mouth?"

The answer was violent, threatening, and leapt from Everett's mouth without his consent. Finding himself staggering, he sat at the kitchen table to compose himself. Breathing heavily, he drank from his beer and stared into the can, very visibly slipping into a reflective state.

"All you kids do is play music. Play, play, play."

Buck's response was defensive and sharp.

"We've got real management, a label paying for studio time. We're still alive."

Only able to ignore the comment, Everett's answer was a mumble.

"We're going fix your sister's car. That's what it is. You kids are going to grow up, start a real life."

"Like you?"

The phone rang. The phone continued to ring. Tension built with the sound of each ring.

Everett was betrayed by his drunken confusion, his spent temper. He found half a cigarette in the ashtray sitting before him and fumbled for a light. Buck decided to leave well enough alone, a perfect lull and opportunity to go, slowly crossing the small kitchen as the phone still insisted to be answered.

With the jolt of frightened action, Everett jumped to his feet.

"Where the hell are you going?" "To look for Piper."

His anger regained its fire with the sound of her name, and instantly his voice was a violent shout. "Are you telling me what it is?"

Buck shouted back.

"Everett, let's not fight."

Standing in Buck's face, Everett's speech was scary, he'd gained an eerie control to his anger and movements.

"Then, why'd you start one?"

Taking exaggerated puffs on his cigarette, Everett built up a big cherry. Buck stood in his spot and reacted as little as he could. He thought to bolt to the door, but Everett came even closer.

"You respect me, understand that. Do you get it?" He extended the cigarette toward Buck.

"Take this."

"I . . . I don't want it."

"I'll tell you what you want, now take it."

Feeling as small as he ever had, Buck's hand took the cigarette, he held it like a foreign object, away from his face, dodging the smoke. Blowing on the cherry, Everett's voice was an evil taunt.

"Don't you want to smoke that?"

Buck's body became inoperable, he couldn't move or think. Catching him by the wrist, Everett looked his son square in the eye. Extending his other arm between them, he exposed his forearm.

"Then, put it out."

Moving Buck's hand with a quick unrelenting force, Everett pushed the cigarette toward his own bare arm.

"You put that right . . . . put it out, right here."

Increasing his grip, Everett's voice was now a low growl. "I'll show you who you're dealing with."

Buck's answer was the shriek of a small child. "It'll burn you, let go!"

Navigating the cigarette, still in Buck's hand, Everett ground the smoke into his own arm firmly. Anything Buck could have offered as resistance had been stripped from him by the caustic absurdity of the act, the demented intent. Everett smiled with the satisfying infliction of pain, and held Buck's hand in position long after the cigarette was out, a smell of sick smoke floating between them.

"I'll tell you what it is . . . anytime."

13

"Anthony, watch the fence. Watch that fence, Anthony."
Immediately Buck grabbed his whistle, blowing three short,
loud, piercing blasts. Standing in a playground full of children
five to ten years old, Buck was at work. This was a private
after school day-care, and children were running and playing
independently all around.

He worked from just after three until about eight, five
days a week. It had been a long bus ride from FW to the top
of Queen Anne, but now he was staying at The Wild's new
practice pad in Georgetown, a placed dubbed studio 420, and
it was a whole lot easier to get to work. The pad had a shower
and everything but it got cold at night, and the noise of other
bands echoed out at all hours.

The last couple months he didn't let himself think about
his father, or anything but work, the band, and getting a place.
He read the apartments-for-rent section like the blueprint to
a breakout. To save enough bread to get his own place was
another eon or so at least, then there was his Mustang still
sitting on blocks down at Everett's.

Bones was hooked up with this kid named Lance from
Canada. Lance was one of the kids that made their money

running grass into this country from up north. The wheel-man on the American side, Bones would drive his stock '69 Chevy up by the border.

He'd wait at a pre-arranged location. Then Lance, a friend or two, sometimes in a group, sometimes staggered, and sometimes solo, would start running with a backpack through the thick evergreen woods of Canada. They'd run for the money.

That morning was Buck's first run.

By the time he and Lance reclined in the back of Bones's Chevelle, their backpacks in the trunk, they were rocket-high on adrenaline, invincible, and back in America, where all that weed in their sacks was worth way more. Not the colored funny money from up north, real greenbacks. Cash.

To make it worth everybody's effort, they moved a lot of product. In this scenario, no one had to manufacture, they simply muled a lot of weed, today it was though miles of thick woods, over a fence, out from someone's backyard and into Bones's Chevy. This was considered new school work, as the Canadian invasion had been in its infancy less than a decade ago.

British Columbia was vying to become the world's new Amsterdam. Soon after it started, it was sending tons of killer greenbud flowing over the border. Shipments came any way they could get it here; cars, boats and trains, Buck, Lance and their fast feet.

This was a magic time of his life and he knew it. Living at

420, there was some kind of party to have all the time, and the rest was work on his voice and lyrics. An eternal insomniac, he could fire up the gear anytime of night and practice not chewing on the mike.

When he was a kid, Everett would make it home just after two regularly. Listening to the crash and stumble of his arrival was where Buck learned to really hear, honing his ear, discerning how loaded, just how dangerous it was to be awake. So late night had always meant peace to him, tucked away in his own world while the rest of everybody slept it off.

A small girl tugged at Buck's shirt. He gave her partial attention by placing his hand on her head. But he remained focused primarily on Anthony.

"Anthony, you need to come here now. Here. Right now." Buck turned to the little girl, who was still tugging. She held a stocking cap in her hand and presented it to him. Buck looked down and directly at her.

"Yes, that is a hat, Amber. Is that your hat?" The little girl shook her head no.

"Did you find that hat, Amber? Yes? Well, you put it back where you found it, 'cause someone may look for it. Ok?"

Looking in the direction of Anthony, he blew a long stout whistle.

"Anthony. Front and center right now. I'm starting a count-down, Anthony."

Amber still extended Buck the hat persistently. "Alright, I'll put it in the lost and found. Thank you, Amber. Outside time is almost over and we are going inside to sing. Ok? . . . very good then."

He took the hat and placed it in his pocket in time to greet a young and rowdy child, exuding enthusiasm.

"Anthony, what did we say about the fence there, fella?" Anthony searched for the right answer with a look to the ground, avoiding Buck's confrontation. "What did we say?"

"We said that I was not to climb on the fence."

"What was that, Anthony? I couldn't hear you." "We said that I was not to climb on the fence."

Buck bent to a knee so that he was eye level with Anthony. "What were you on the fence for?"

"I was climbing it."

Just then, back by the tether-ball poles, Piper and Skyler entered from the far end of the pavement. Each carried a backpack. Leaning against one another other in a slow stroll, they crossed the playground toward Buck, who was finishing with little Anthony.

"Well, you've got to be careful of fences, tough guy."

Buck stood to greet Piper and Skyler, dismissing Anthony with an absent pat to head.

"Alright, hotshot, hit the road."

Anthony ran off to play. His arm around Piper, and with a wink to Sky, Buck blew his whistle officially. Showboating for his friends, he shouted a general announcement to the playground with a voice that mocked every authority.

"Outside time is almost over, let's get ready to go inside for choir."

Everyone, all the kids, started putting stuff away, the ropes in the box, the balls in a large mesh bag.

"Let's move it, move, move."

His cheap Patton imitation kick-started kids buzzing around. Organized and effective, they briskly packed up the playground. Buck's attention was suddenly caught and he went for his whistle with a long loud blast.

"Anthony, you come down from there right now . . . Yes, I know that is a tree, Anthony. You come down right now." Blowing his whistle louder, he made another general announcement.

"Alright everyone line up, outside time is over. Everyone line up . . . Anthony, you get the front of the line . . ."

He lightly put a hand on the beaming child's shoulder, guiding him to the front to the line.

". . . because you're brave Anthony, that's why." Children ran from all corners of the playground and started to line up behind Anthony. Quickly, and in single file, they waited for

Buck to give out the next cue. Piper greeted Buck with a kiss to his cheek.

A week ago Friday was the last time he'd seen her. The Wild rehearsed three days a week and ran their set the day they played a show. It was the only time she came to Seattle anymore, when they played, and Buck wondered what the deal was.

"Hey guys, you remember my sister, Piper." All the kids shouted back in unison.

"Hi, Piper!"

Directing the line to face them, Buck clapped his hands demanding serious attention.

"Hey, everybody remember our song?"

There was an assortment of answers, all indicating the affirmative.

"Ready? . . . One, two, three . . ."

The children started humming first, with Buck conducting. The second time through, the melody had entranced them, and with a sweeping gesture on Buck's part, the kids kicked in. Most any large group of young voices can have an appealing sound, but these kids had been working with Buck for months, the first wave of their song was angelic.

"Smile child, Prayer for the Wild . . ."

The chorus was cut into a round of thirds, the second section starting with the next line.

"Sing me a song . . ."

Then the third followed suit. "Let the smile shine awhile . . ."

The group continued weaving the lyric and sound as Buck, still conducting, let his voice fly above them with a verse.

". . . Oh Yeah, mother mother Mary, she cries every night and says it's time to share me . . ."

It was a fluid groove with an the edge of funk that he laid on top of the soft sound. He sang with a razor edge to his voice and a powerful drive to the end of the line. The lilting pad of the children's chorus behind him enhanced the dynamic, an opposition, that each sound thrived in, and he continued to the second line of verse.

". . . Said pure love is pulling me to sound, I'm an open mind super-wild, cherry pie love child . . ."

That much was in stone, virtually the same with every version, the rest of the words were anybody's guess. Like so many major influences, much of it was indecipherable, but all of it carried impact. Lightening his tone, Buck directed the kids into one voice, ending the round, and then joined them as they all ended together on the last line of chorus.

". . . sing me a song, let the smile shine a while."

Swinging his arm gently in rhythm, he conducted them all to a soft stop. It was Piper's wry smile that told Buck everything, she liked it as much as he did. They talked about using a chorus of kids as an intro to the tune, perhaps a preamble of sorts, but now Piper wanted them for the whole song.

"What do you think?"

"Got to get you kids into the studio."

Skyler agreed with a steady nod of his head. Inhaling a deep satisfaction, Buck turned to the kids and dismissed them into the building. He held the door open, repeating instructions as they filed along.

"Thanks guys, everyone leaving at six has to get ready to go. Everybody else, let's hang up our things when we get inside." As the door slammed, the kids were gone. Skyler gripped Buck by his shoulders. He expressed with his eyes what he knew his words might lack, how much he cherished what he'd just heard.

"That was really good Buck, really."

The response was strangely avid, but Buck could tell it was an honest expression. Bones had listened to the kids weeks ago, and he dug it too. Buck was pumped that everyone was into his contribution, and he reaped a palpable satisfaction by merging several parts of his life into something positive and of apparent quality.

"Well, I'm glad you guys like it. I already got releases from all their parents. If we record them, it's ours, we could use it live."

Piper spoke up.

"Oh, yeah, and certainly on the album." "Album?"

"It's going to happen, Buck, right around the corner."

"You got to angle before you can land."

Small bumps raced over his skin and a wave surged down his spine tingling every nerve. He'd been scared they'd lost momentum after moving from the garage. It had taken over a month to get a new routine established, and even more recently Buck had deciphered that there was some strange distraction in Piper's usual unwavering focus.

Never asking about the state of the deal, careful not to press about or bother, build anxiety or expectation, Buck had become silently concerned that Piper might be thinking she made a mistake by putting so much faith in him. He knew they might be close to closing something up, The Wild's last two shows were stuffed with industry stiffs, and if there was some kind of holdup he didn't want to be it.

Any doubts were left behind when he saw her response to his extra-credit project, the choir, and his voice. Piper was easy to read, she couldn't hide anything from him, and she was. To Buck it was obvious some issue, some obstacle had been preying on her mind and occupying time.

She had met every requirement of the band; still called the shots, ripped up all the shows, even found and negotiated the practice room. That was all real easy for her to do. There was something else, and with his worries about himself soothed, his mind was left to wonder what else might be wrong.

"Hey, we got shoes for Piper's Colt and we're going to take off over east of the mountains 'til Tuesday."

Whatever it was, Skyler knew all about it.

"We'll get down to it next week, Friday is going to be our last show without a label, and we're going to have to make some tough decisions."

Her voice still had that fire when she talked about the band, maybe it was just something between those two. It was real obvious that relationships and band members had never seemed a perfect scenario, there were plusses and minuses. Buck tried to figure if it was some subtraction, or an impending addition, that was bothering his sister so.

"Are you sure everything is cool?"

"Everything is cool."

The ease in her voice told him that it was something serious, and he saw the same thing on Skyler.

"See you."

The last two words slipped past her smile and she embraced her brother, leaving him with a kiss to his cheek. A powerful sensation crept over Buck, and weakened his knees as he watched them walk into the distance. Suddenly he felt light and nauseous and noticed a warm sensation on his upper lip.

Wiping at his face, he was startled by the sight of blood on the back on his hand. He pinched the bridge of his nose and angled his head back. Grabbing the doorknob to go, he glanced to his left, and the sight froze his every muscle.

Buck watched as Piper and Skyler went back the way they came. One leaned against another other in a slow stroll, moving across the playground. They passed the tether-ball poles, jumped the fence, and headed back into the city.

It was the last time anyone who loved Skyler James or Piper Wild would see them alive.

14

The ringing started shortly after sunrise.

It was so early that Everett, passed out in his chair, couldn't even consider answering the first forty times it rang. But it kept sounding off, ringing and ringing, knocking on his consciousness, becoming increasingly agitating until finally his arm came to a fumbling life, blindly searching for the phone. His hand found the receiver, held it up to his ear, and he answered with a dry rasp.

Eyes slowly opened as Everett listened. His morning fog was thick, leaving him thirsty and confused. He was sure it must be one of his dreams.

Like a distant sound of thunder, an approaching storm, three quick startling gun shots and sound of screams melded into in his mind. He listened to what was said on the other end of line, and the information being relayed smacked him in the face. When this new reality began to register, the phone dropped from his hand to the floor, and he fell sick.

It was hours later he found himself halfway down the hallway to the bathroom, and he wondered just what had been a dream, and what was real. Too many thoughts had free reign in his tired skull, and it was time to make it to the kitchen. A great effort brought Everett to the counter by the fridge, and he took survey of last night's trail.

Cluttered cans gave way to the real culprit, a clear plastic gallon container with a red and blue label proclaiming a brand name in Russian. Everett immediately shot bubbles into what was the last of the liquid. Momentarily satiated in the early glow it produced, he kept it in hand and found a chair, to sit and think.

The phone started again, and he gave it a weary look, letting it ring. The repetitive noise drove into his head, it was just more news to be avoided. How does one listen to that?

He drank, and when he was good and loaded, Everett called the Pine household and asked for Jeff. Bones's mother recognized the rough-edged voice, the slurred speech as Everett, and asked what the issue was. Reacting with a dull snap he told her, if she saw her kid, to tell Buck it was imperative he call home immediately.

"You mean, call you, right?"

She'd heard the latest full story and had been again persuaded not to pursue anything legal by Bones's insistence that it wasn't her business, and in the end, it would do more harm than good. Over the years she'd seen Everett in all states, and she absolutely believed him to be an unsound person, no kind of a parent, and had even been personally threatened by him on several accounts. This last tale of the escalated violence, Sky's short stay in the hospital, her extended love for Buck, and a real fear for her own child, had all left the quietly religious woman with the brutal notion that Everett had the devil in him, a demon, and the children, the world, might be better off without him.

Even still, as she hung up, she was sure something was seriously wrong, something more than the desperate drunk and his attempt to reconcile with an abused son was going on. She'd taken many, many, of those calls, and after repeatedly apologizing for the inconvenience, Buck told her to ignore them, he didn't even want to hear about it. But this time there had been a shake in the voice, a shattering quality that scared her.

Everett's insistence of how important the news was, and his long silences between speech, convinced her to write a note. Her lacy cursive reminded Jeff of a dental appointment on Thursday, and told him to get Buck to call his father immediately. Placing the paper on front of the refrigerator, the only spot Bones was sure to see it, she left in a hurry for a late afternoon lunch date.

It was later that week Buck finally phoned Everett. He'd known what his father had to tell him for three days, the whole city did. It'd been the front page of the living section.

Buck had heard the news first from Shwetty, a soft-spoken forty-something rocker who played in a hair-band named Painted Nails, a tribute, cover-song outfit, that Shwetty gigged in for fun, and to retain a core of his personal identity. Otherwise, he made a life renting practice rooms to bands out of his old warehouse in Georgetown. The only other live-in occupant of the place was now Buck.

When Shwetty saw the paper that morning he fell into tears. After about fifteen minutes of sobbing, a huge choker of a bong hit, and a few moments sitting in silence, he collected himself and walked to studio 420. He'd stayed up into the early morning with Buck partying, and had only about three hours of rest under his belt, so if Buck was still asleep in the studio, there was no way he could know what he was about to find out.

Shwetty wasn't sure if he was the exact right person. But someone had to do it, to be the first to say the words. Having been a good friend for a long time, he felt it would be best not to have Buck see something in the paper, or walk out into a world that was about to flood him with questions.

Rubbing his thinning hair in stress, he gathered a smoke from his pocket, and knocked on the door as a blanket of guilt began to smother him, as if he had done, or was about to do, a horrible thing himself. Indeed the message he bore would lay waste to his young friend. There was no doubt life had changed forever.

Shwetty patted himself down for a light, gave fire to the cigarette with a deep drag, and stood by the door waiting to knock. He was wise enough to know that the way this was done would be carried around forever, this moment. A musician and life-long artist, Shwetty had garnered a large dose of new-age sentimentally as he'd gained years.

He looked to the ceiling and made a cognitive recognition that what was before him was a spiritual charge. To have the courage to tell Buck, to be there. To pad, if he could, the beginning of what was bound to be a long haul to a most challenging end.

Stirring at the persistent knocking, Buck roused himself from the couch, undid the latch and scurried back to the warmth of his sleeping bag. It was obvious that Shwetty was all shook up about something, so Buck gave a stretch and tried to be attentive. What he heard blew his world away.

Countless questions raced to be answered, and as Shwetty retrieved the Times, everything Buck was ran to ice. He stared without expression at the news, asked if he could keep the paper, and then to be left alone. Convinced he had contributed to keeping it calm, Shwetty agreed that if anyone asked, no one had seen Buck, or knew where he was.

The door to Studio 420 stayed shut the rest of the day and into the next morning. It was only answered when Buck recognized Bones's knock. The report from the outer world was just as he read in the paper.

Everything seemed to be so far from reality. Bones said the story had been reported on the news last night, and that only Robert had been reached for a statement. Nobody answered at the Wild residence, not the phone or the front door.

The bereaved Mrs. Pine hired a service for Sky's funeral. It was a huge affair attended by a wide swath of social classes. Half the enormous church was filled with suits and formal attire, the other half had arrived in ripped denim and leather, all were awash in mourning.

Every person present had known Skyler James. When one was around Sky, touched by his presence, the beautiful ease he possessed with himself and the world around him, it left an indelible impression. Today that bond had gathered all these people together.

A select list of folks had been asked to speak. Buck declined, but agreed to sing. Bones was the last to talk about his friend before the minister was to take the pulpit and it all became by the numbers.

"Meet him once, remember him forever. Sky was like that."

Bones had worn a faded muscle shirt displaying his tattoos, to honor his friend, even though Skyler had never so much as pierced an ear, let alone gotten any ink. It was the unfettered spirit, the raw rebel soul, Bones wished to represent, to sanctify. So he did his hair up in a sharp spike, painted thick dark circles around his eyes, and tucked the legs of his faded black jeans into the steel-toed motorcycle boots he'd bought on Skyler's advice, to protect himself in any potentially sticky situation.

"Kick someone with those, they'll know all about it, Bones."

With a reverence that captured the room, Jeff softly recalled accounts of the person he'd come to revere. He explained that he believed people like Skyler are here to light the course of our lives, a rare illumination he cherished every time he'd been in Sky's presence. A single soiled tear fell from his blackened eye and found its way down the side of his face.

"So goodbye, Sky, I'll never ever forget you, or the music we made."

Defiantly, Bones thrust his fist in to the air and held it there, finishing with two simple words.

"Life rules."

As he stepped down, the church was dead silent. With a wise smile, the preacher kindly motioned for Buck to sing. He realized anything said in words would be less than trivial.

With some shaking air, Buck's breath hit the words and he began to sing 'Amazing Grace.' The song and his mourning voice matched the mood, filled the space, and for a stanza he sang by himself. Then Bones and a small group in the front left joined in, and it took only a couple more lines for the rest of the room to sing.

Never again would this group of people be so close to Skyler's memory, to the time that he lived, or to that time in their own lives. As they sang, they shared the truth of human mortality, a sadness and celebration. Understood was the fleeting frailty and enduring notion of something so beautiful as the flower of a single human life.

And then the song was over.

There'd been no mention of Piper at the proceedings, not a word.

Claire, the reporter, now writing for a national feed, re-ran her interview with Piper, with the revised title: 'Last talk with a local legend?' She included an extensive foreword explaining how deeply she'd been impacted by the music, and later by the person. It went on at length, mentioning Skyler, and then the band, telling about how close The Wild was to being signed, how good they were, how they had promised to be the future of Rock and Roll.

She took the saga to a friend at the local television station who was more than receptive to the idea of a doing a spotlight on the story. Using an assortment of Piper's images, words and music, even her voice, taken from Claire's interview tape and used in a narrative, they created a video that recounted the facts in a most sensational way. It ended with a one-eight-hundred number asking for anyone who might have seen Piper to call.

People called, mostly to ask if they could buy a tape of the broadcast, or just to express some sentiment to someone they thought might listen. But nobody knew what happened, where Piper was. Weeks became a month and the buzz began to grow.

When Buck finally called Everett, the phone rang into eternity without an answer. Taking the bus to Federal Way was the longest ride of his life, and when he exited at the park-n-ride, the wet walk to Diamond Jack's seemed just as long. Like a prophecy, there was Everett seated in the far corner of the lounge.

Usually he hated being tracking down, but Everett smiled at the sight of his son. Half the patrons knew Buck from countless occasions, and he was greeted by Del who pierced him with his eyes. The round bartender grabbed Buck by the shoulders and in a deep bass quietly expressed his concern.

"Where the hell have you been, Buck?"

Without waiting for a response he gave him a huge hug, slapping Buck on the back, and laughing.

"You promised to come here for your first legal drink, you're late."

Then Del pointed him in the direction of Everett, and with the help of a slight shove, Buck cautiously approached the corner. Despite what he'd deemed as the better part of himself, the part that had promised never to speak to this bastard again, the sight of his father lifted a weight that had been sitting inside him. Turning the chair backward, he sat down directly in front of Everett with a silent tongue, his face held in a stoic mask.

The span between them was comprised of much more than miles. A flickering red candle glowed on the table, and then waved brightly from the wind as Del abruptly sat a beer before Buck and marched away again. In silence Buck observed the fizz and bubbles of his gift.

What does one let go of? What's to keep? What is an issue, an answer, or just an endless bunch of questions?

Everett could see the race of thoughts and the amount of emotion in his son, and knew it was a reflection of himself. Sometimes it comes down to the truth of a moment, and regardless of what may seem any great number of ways, indifferent of our dreams, hopes, plans and potential, at any given second, we are what we are. We do what we do.

The frost from the glass stung his hand. Buck held it up, the dim light of the lounge hit the sparkling liquid and he admired its perfect color; he swallowed half of it in a drink, the cold suds flowed into his body, as did a wave of relieved satisfaction. Everett remembered to search his pockets, and quickly he retrieved a small round ring with two keys.

"Got your Mustang off the blocks and running, new battery, some tires."

For a little bit the world was somewhere else. Del brought more drinks and beers and both of them talked about things that made everything seem just fine. Soon it was after two and they made the short stagger across the street, down a block, and ducked behind the grocery store to the spot where Everett had parked his Cadillac.

It was there, as the car belched a frozen cloud into the air, warming to life with a wheezing chug, that they first dared to slur into the topic indelibly ingrained into their lives. Out of a dead silence it was Everett who spoke first. His words brought home a sting of reality, a somber sense of sobriety.

"Can you believe it? . . . Why?"

His whisper wasn't able to conceal the depth of his loss, his devastated awe. It was the soft shaking voice of a man talking to one of the last living confidants he had, to a friend. He lifted his head to meet Buck's watering eyes.

"What the hell are we supposed to do now?"

Buck suddenly felt more like a grown-up than he ever had. That was the very question hammering in his own head, and for Everett not to offer any comfort or solution, but to heave the burden of a response, scared Buck in the deepest pit of his stomach. A glacier of reality was about him and he wanted to cry, then realized he already was.

His father had been made a real human, for perhaps the first time. Not a hero or a monster. He was just a person, more frail than most.

Responding to the fire inside, Buck made the concentrated and willful decision to problem-solve, to get mad, to attack. His fist gave a quick pound to the dash and then he pulled at the back of his hair, and ground his teeth with a clenched jaw. He demanded one answer from himself.

What would Piper say?

Get a plan of attack, some solid action, hearing her voice in his head, Buck used the words he thought she might.

"Well, what do you think our options are?"

Attempting a slow climb out of their mire of confusion, alcohol, and grief, they talked in circles until the Cadillac had eaten a half-tank. When they finally merged onto Highway 99, each vowed to do whatever it was they could do. Their mental list began at conferring with an attorney, and then a private investigator.

Certainly the press was to be part of Everett and Buck's plan. But it happened, before they could even begin to figure out how it might be done. The popular and charismatic host of a highly-rated network television show was sitting in their front room.

Jacklyn was fresh from deep in the heart of Hollywood, California. Just a week before, one of her story finders, a demographic specialist, high in a large building of darkened glass emblazoned with a neon logo consisting of three red letters, became impressed with the numbers in response to a local Northwest spot called 'Last look at a local legend?' When presented with the story, Jacklyn instantly wanted to help.

Of course she noted the cross-over appeal, the drama the story conveyed, and decided it would be a perfect segment for their season opener.

15

"Welcome Home."

Jacklyn Wright was a one-time school-teaching nobody from San Diego, California. Her life had been transformed decades earlier, when she'd left her four-year-old sitting in front of a video game display and browsed vacuums on the next aisle over. She was out of direct eye contact with the child for an approximate total of six minutes.

Over the next seven weeks, pieces of her son were found in three adjacent counties. The gruesome details of the abduction, and Jacklyn's exhaustive search were recounted in a made-for-television melodrama that generated significant acclaim, and was credited for revising statutes and procedures across the country. Jacklyn was the recipient of an instant notoriety and made rounds on all the talk shows.

The format she pitched for her own show to the network was, at the time, cutting-edge. Missing person stories, reenactments, and one-eight-hundred numbers for the masses to call in with information, accounts, and tips. The show was titled 'Welcome Home,' and was an instant hit.

It was one of the first true crime based shows, a main groundbreaker into what was to become the reality television wave. Jacklyn gained a powerful celebrity and quickly became the champion and defender of America's missing. She grew into a slick and experienced professional, projecting a seamless, refined, almost regal image.

Starting community watch programs and spearheading judicial reforms, she also worked with industry players on several spin-off shows, including one to track down wanted criminals, and recently another apprising the world of threatening terrorist organizations. Jacklyn Wright had received endless local awards from all around the country. She garnered three Emmy's, and the vocal praise of two Presidents. "I'm Jacklyn Wright."

When she spoke, it was with an agitated clip, and an indignant righteousness, the trumpet of her phrasing was often at odds with the rounded relaxed tones of her voice, helping render her a distinct and unique delivery she became noted for. A tall woman with a mountain of dark brown hair, she was stylish yet conservative, and wore sparse makeup highlighting her light graceful features. Her stylist tended to want to dress her in soft pastels while she leaned toward bold primary colors, as a result her wardrobe usually landed somewhere in the middle.

"Tonight, we are in the home of Everett Wild. Sitting next to Everett is his son, Everett junior."

"Call me Buck."

The house was full of cords, lights, equipment, and a crew of eight. A simulated oasis of Norman Rockwell Americana had been blatantly staged in the otherwise cluttered and trashed home, complete with freshly cut flowers, a tasteful sofa, chair, and matching coffee cups. The prop couch was the centerpiece of this manufactured set, warmly lit with an inviting amber, tastefully angled in front of the window, with the lake glimmering in the background.

"Everett, we're here today to investigate the disappearance of Piper Wild, your oldest child and only daughter."

"That's correct, Jacklyn." "The facts are this."

The words stung Buck's ears, and Everett stopped listening.

"Skyler James, reported boyfriend and band-mate of your daughter Piper, was found thirty meters off a deserted desert section of interstate ninety, in Eastern Washington."

The interview was shot with three cameras claiming close-ups, a series of two-shots, and one master of the set.

"There were definite signs of a struggle."

It would all be put together in post later, edited with a grab bag of actual crime scene and location shots, stills and visuals, sound effects and music, that were showing on a large monitor in the room to incite appropriate reaction shots.

"An apparent John Doe victim of what was obviously a horrible homicide, he'd been unnoticed for days, perhaps a week, until two mountain-bikers found the slain Skyler James."

Finally the whole segment would be mixed to the baseline of Jacklyn's feminine, yet staccato baritone, as she recounted the facts with the feel of a preview, or promotional spot, for the anticipated release of an upcoming blockbuster.

"Skyler James had been shot three times."

Sweeping footage of the crime scene shot from a helicopter rendered a huge overview of a remote and desolate area.

"Injures from two of the bullets left him unidentifiable for days after he was found, until partial dental records proved who it was."

A photograph of Skyler faded to the image of his lifeless legs, a cropped version of an official police photo, his low-cut tennis shoes propped against the guitar case in an unnatural twist.

"Left beside Skyler was this guitar case."

A heavy-set production assistant, with cargo pants and a headset, brought the case in, and handed it to Everett in front of the rolling cameras. Outwardly his reaction was stoic, solid, he took a look at the guitar, shook his head to the side, and handed it to Buck. Truth was, the sight had pushed him right up to the point of breaking, his breath was short and labored, his vision slightly blurred, and he felt altogether nauseous.

He glanced again at the case Buck held in his arms and noticed the side was slightly damaged. When had that happened? Some load out, some show?

Or had it been part of the fight? Become a weapon when she needed it to? Had it been her last line of defense against an attacker?

On the request of Ms. Wright, Buck opened the case. It was the sort of instrument one hears on sight. The guitar was fine, cradled contentedly in the soft orange fuzzy lining, snapped into place with two worn leather straps, across the neck and body, that Everett had installed himself.

"Written inside, the name Piper Wild, and this address." A close-up of the guitar case revealed name and address inscribed on a small gold-colored plate inside.

"It has been confirmed by eyewitnesses, who reportedly are the last to talk to the two at a convenience store in Issaquah, that they were heading over the pass to Eastern Washington for the weekend."

Two actors playing Piper and Skyler drove a Dodge Colt, similar to Piper's, but in better shape and washed.

"As authorities continue to put the pieces together, the picture tends to tell of Piper's vehicle running into automotive difficulties."

Dimly lit re-enactment footage showed the two actors driving the Colt, a cloud of steam emanating from under the hood.

"It appears the two were able to drive the sputtering wreck, in the dead of night, off the road to the last freeway rest stop before Vantage, Washington, the very same parking lot where the car was later found, abandoned."

Blasts from the actors' breath into the freezing air, and their hitchhiking thumbs, were used as cutaways and close-ups as the two walked along a narrow strip of path beside the rest stop, from the Colt to the freeway entrance.

"Morning came early and still in the cover of darkness, it is presumed the two started back to the interstate, and according to official speculation, began to hitchhike."

An abrupt and stylized dramatization of a fight was staged. The dark and silhouetted sequence ended with three quick, startling gunshots. A shadowed aggressor left the actor playing Skyler bleeding on the ground, then snatched the young actress as she screamed in a flail.

"Not far from the rest stop, out of earshot, perhaps a hundred yards, police found spent shells and signs of a struggle between what they claim was probably three people."

The visuals ended with the repeat image of Skyler, his lifeless low-cut tennis shoes and the guitar case.

"Chances are wherever Piper's gone, she didn't want to go there. Is that about it, Everett?"

"Yes."

At the end of her line, the visuals returned to Jacklyn, then her close-up widened to include Everett and Buck.

"That is the story as you know it, then, Everett?" "That's what we've come to understand, Jacklyn."

Jacklyn shifted camera, tempo, and tactic, and the in-room monitor continued to show much of what would be edited in later to develop continuity and provoke emotion.

"Piper Wild is a dynamic young lady from a unique family."

A picture of a young and impressive Everett filled the screen.

"Her father, Everett Wild, carved out a niche as guitarist and songwriter, hired on a list of favorites as a studio player, and grabbed the glory by penning one sentimental hit everyone remembers, 'Touch of Grace,' a song that reigned on the charts in its time, and is still heard on classic and oldies stations today."

Smiling softly, Everett answered Jacklyn.

"Country was big enough to have a lot of one-hit wonders, Jacklyn. It was a long time ago."

"Grace Wild, your late wife, was also a musician?"

"She's been gone for many years." "A singer, she was a singer."

Buck's interjection was coupled with a photograph of Grace, as a young woman. She had that same smile. The obvious family resemblance was highlighted as the monitor switched to a promotional shot of Piper playing her guitar onstage.

"Piper Wild is a young lady who defined herself at sixteen, as a founding member of the all-girl punk band, Diary."

Footage and live shots of Diary played as a visual, while a medley of their music created a moving background bed for Jacklyn's omnipotent narrative.

"Local favorites, Diary was among the first of a slough of local bands that landed recording deals."

Diary's first album cover was highlighted. On the cover was a slightly blurred snapshot of the three girls sitting on top of the hood of an olive green Duster, under a streetlight, parked against a brick wall, in an industrial part of Tacoma. The hood of the rig and the girls were in the right foreground, Piper in the middle, the rest of the alley was angled off behind them at a hard diagonal.

It was a candid shot taken after a show. Whoever took the picture had mailed it to the band in a large express envelope. Enclosed along was a slightly torn pair of peach colored panties and a one-word note, 'Thanks.'

No one ever owned up to knowing anything more about the picture or the panties. But the band decided it was the perfect representation of their life and times, and the picture was just fine for the cover. The album was self-titled in scrawling hot pink letters across the bottom, 'Diary.'

"A seminal part of a musical movement, Diary cemented their place into the foundation of the local scene. Just ask their still avid fans, and music experts alike."

Behind the counter of an independent music store, the owner, Gerald, a highly intelligent, dark-skinned dude with mutton chops and thick-rimmed dork glasses, matriculated his answer in deep and confident bass tones.

"Well that's the thing, isn't it? You listen to them now, the time test, you know?"

He held up the Diary disk, then turned to push play on the stereo behind him, and music leapt quickly to life. "And then, ask yourself."

As the song started, a look of great discernment crept onto Gerald's face, then, when the raw guitar lead ripped the music into its first full refrain, he moved his head to the rhythm with a knowing nod, a certified satisfaction.

"Yeah. You know? You can hear it."

It grew louder and the visual switched to the violating bright of cheap video. The crude shots of Diary playing back in the day, of ecstatic screaming fans, had a dated but edgy look. The image switched to a modern-day digital close-up of an engrossed and highly-informed Jacklyn Wright.

"The brutal slaying of Skyler James, and Piper Wild's disappearance, has stunned fans and rocked this tight-knit music community."

Current media files showed a mid-sized crowd of shocked
fans, mourners, and well-wishers, assembled on the sidewalk
outside a club. Stacks of flowers were framing a brilliant
mass of candles and the flickering flame that lit pictures of
Piper, her bands, and Skyler, all decoratively propped up as a
memorial. A slight young teen with a stoned sneer, a tight black
tank top, and a shock of short spiky blonde, voiced his opinion
in a head-and-shoulders shot.

"Um, I really want them to release The Wild stuff. But,
yeah, of course, I'm a major fan of Diary. What's cool is they
were never freeze-dried for export, you know?"

The shot widened to include an interloper into the
interview with an identical viewpoint, and a similar outfit.
"Yeah, see, that's it, they're still ours."

Jacklyn continued her seamless narrative.

"Every record deal doesn't necessarily mean millions."

The frame found a beleaguered Robert slumped behind
his desk, smoking.

"With Diary, we were still learning the business. There is
just so much more to a band than music."

A quick-cut series of clips ended up on a young Piper in
punk attire standing next to a club long gone, yelling directly
into the camera over the sound of the party behind her.

"Diary's a chapter for the books, man. The right kids,
people who love music, they'll find us, our music, again and
again, we're here forever."

Over a selection of pictures, taken in the last several
years, Jacklyn gave second—and third-hand accounts of Piper's
recent antics. She recounted that Piper played lead tracks on
several local bands' demos, a few gigs, did a small tour with
an old Canadian punk band that had a brief popular revival,
and that she was also arrested year before last, twice, for third-
degree assault. Jacklyn's speech ended on the only promotional
picture of The Wild, a live shot taken during a show in Ballard.

"But when she founded The Wild, many felt they were witnessing something extraordinary."

Standing against a stream of people piling out of a concrete-colored door, a trendy hipster in a crushed brown fedora leaned against his gum-chewing girlfriend and was more prophetic than he knew.

"The Wild is it. Fifteen years from now, we'll be all be saying 'I was there,' or 'I saw them play this tiny club.'"

The cool drawl of the hipster created a jarring contrast to Jacklyn's sober image and somber statement.

"But it seems now The Wild's song has come to an unexpected end."

Filing out a backstage door into a dank and drizzling alley, Piper was caught in the candid crosshairs of a digital camera. She flashed a peace sign with her right hand. Skyler came up from behind, scooping her in a playful hug.

His profile was partially shrouded in the tangle of her long hair as he embraced her cheek with a kiss. Piper loved the attention and her hand touched the side of his face, but the slightest pout played on her proud smile, lost into the camera. The image on the monitor froze in motion, to a still, and then aged slowly to black and white, to a legend.

"Now, let's find Piper, people. If you've seen her, please call our hot tip line immediately."

Jacklyn spoke over the picture until a slow dissolve brought the attention back to a close-up on her.

"Light up those phones, America, and we'll welcome Piper Wild home."

She turned from her close-up camera to the sofa, directing her ending comments to Buck and Everett.

"Thank you, Everett, Buck. Good night and good luck." Jacklyn ended as she did every show, her last line square into the camera.

"This is Jacklyn Wright, Welcome Home."

There was a smattering of applause from the crew, and Jacklyn immediately stood to shake the family's hands.

"Thank you, Gentlemen. Let's keep our fingers crossed." Buck's inquiry came quickly as to catch her attention. "Will they further the investigation after this?"

Distracted by the business of the crew breaking set, dealing with several quick questions, Jacklyn was professional and short, but not without a note of implied real concern.

"Possible follow-up show if people really respond, certainly this segment will see some syndication."

Buck's penetrating stare created a crack in her professional veneer, and she answered him with more than the intonation of irony, something close to sympathy.

"Welcome to show-biz, kid."

16

The whistle blasted its voice across the playground.

An ear-cleaving pitch demanded the swarming children listen and commanded them to store the play-balls, jump-ropes and gear. It was an abrupt and shrill whine that signaled the end of recess. The end of fun.

Lined up single file, the children gathered by the back of the brick building, ready to go inside. Buck walked to the front of the line and stood with his hand on the door. He waited out a moment of ruckus, until he gained their attention and the floor.

"Ok, kids, I think some of you already know the big news on the playground, but here's what it is."

The children were rapt on the edge of Buck's words, perhaps never more serious in their short lives.

"You'll have a new assistant teacher starting tomorrow." There was a mixed reaction amongst the kids ranging from 'told you so' to authentic gasps of sorrow, shock, and disbelief. "I have some important stuff to go do, and I got to get to it."

He opened the door and the children filed past him in a sad procession. Purposefully straggling, Anthony was the last in line, and he came to a full stop in front of Buck. His head was slumped to the side in a pout, slowly he raised his eyes from the blacktop.

"Yes, Anthony?"

"Are you ever coming back?"

Buck answered him with a wry smile.

"No one ever gets to go back kid, it's all forward from here."

He mussed Anthony's hair with affection, and the two walked inside, the large metal door slamming behind them.

17

Looking more like hell every day, Robert had gained weight and started to go really gray.

He would pull through most of his smokes in less than six drags, until they were a soaking, scrunched hot-box with a quarter-inch cherry, from which he would light the next cigarette. A film began to form that covered his skin and clothing. Living in his office, he had too many loose ends to tie up, so many balls in the air.

Buck never had to deal directly with Robert that much before. Seldom was it just the two of them, and rarely had they really spoke. The more than ten year stretch that separated them was compounded by Robert's offsetting adult demeanor and Buck's total encasement in a world of his own.

There was much more than a satisfactory market share response to the 'Welcome Home' segment and every available Diary album in the city was gone. Robert was fielding calls interested in re-releasing anything they cut. Several labels were asking questions about Piper's first band PartyGirl.

Who owned the rights? Where are the masters? Robert was in the middle of what was becoming a mid-sized media wave, and he couldn't help but love it.

Then, when he noticed himself having too much fun, he'd think of Piper, his stomach would hurt, and he would smoke. He really wanted just to work all the time. That's all he'd really wanted to do, more now than ever.

But he couldn't conceive of doing anything, being engaged in any transaction that might tarnish or diminish, or 'sell out' Piper in any way. Artistic sensibilities and such were never his strong suit, not his end, nor did he pretend they were. When anything he was involved in 'sold-out' it meant he'd done his job, and had done it well, the term equaled cash and success to him.

He'd always counted on Piper as his hip-meter, a register of cool, just exactly what was the low down and what was a load. More sublimely and with an even more serious intent he shadowed her stance on political opinion and life issues.

Anyone who knew Piper personally was literally forced to think about the widest array of subjects due to her volume and repetition.

Applying a consistent philosophy, Piper's ideals were rigid in their tolerance, and they only grew more fiercely defined with additional information and further maturation. A relentless American with revolution in her heart, she retained the realistic grounding of someone who'd never had a trust fund. Her intrinsic intelligence and social circumstance had endowed Piper, at no small expense, with an unfailing insight into what was real.

The deepest part of his insides told Robert that the kid sitting in front of him was as close to a comparable moral compass as he could ever hope to find. In most ways, Buck was the direct product of Piper's tutelage, as she immersed him in her personal doctrine from the very beginning. Whatever Buck's upbringing lacked in consistency and convention, with Piper as a big sister, his childhood blossomed with cool.

Buck had put it off, left messages, disappeared and dodged as much as possible. But dealing with Robert was one of several tooth-pulling tasks that now had to get done. First on a list of things to do before leaving town.

There was a phone call from a trucker. He was one of hundreds who watched 'Welcome Home,' and felt compelled to phone in with a tip. He reported seeing a couple fitting Piper and Skyler's description fighting with a man, at the back of a van, pulled over to the side of the road, only a short distance from the rest-stop where the Colt had been found.

To avoid a potential trap, the trucker hadn't stopped, but company records confirmed he reported the sighting to his dispatcher, who supposedly phoned the police. The authorities' files showed no such report, and as a consequence, their official comment demanded that any conflicting information, apparent or perceived negligence, was on the part of the trucking company, and/or the dispatcher herself.

Armed with this new information, Jacklyn Wright pushed for a follow-up show. Her proposal was to organize, and air, an actual search for Piper, at the apparent scene of the crime. In the light of the trucker's story, Jacklyn decided that it was a strong possibility that if Piper had been killed, perhaps her remains were hidden in the rock, dirt, and scotch-broom sprawl of the desert.

Her first impression was that Piper might still be alive. Perhaps she and Skyler parted ways. Maybe she'd been taken, or taken off herself.

But now it seemed a stronger possibility that she'd become a corpse, discarded in the desert. If they could find a body at least the story would be put to rest, the truth would be known. Without a body, the possibilities were too endless, the scenarios too scary.

Logically the best place to start seriously looking was the last place she was. There was a standard and cursory scan of the general area when Skyler had been found. But now it demanded a real, full-on, exhaustive search.

On the freeway overpass, walking to meet Robert, Buck leaned on the guardrail watching I-5 stream below him.

Listening to the rush of traffic, he made the difficult decision to take part in the search. Finding a payphone he told Jacklyn's office that he'd handle his own transportation, and would most probably be out of touch until the day of the search, the shoot, next week, when he'd meet them there.

"Well, what do you plan to do?"

It occurred to Buck that Robert didn't know about the upcoming additional 'Welcome Home' segment or his impending trip across the mountains to take part in the show, so he told him. After a crawling pause, Robert began to speak methodically.

"Buck, Piper and I were . . ."

His eyes shot to Buck's, who answered him with a forced and tight lipped smile.

". . . are partners. I booked her first show. We've always been good friends."

Everything he said felt forced. Sounded like the things one should say. He stretched his limited ability to express himself and found words that rang with the truth and feeling he was attempting to convey.

"Piper and I, we . . . we're smarter together than we ever will be apart."

His next statement was a confession, and bridged his thoughts back to the release, the emotional and intellectual permission, he wanted from Buck.

"I've been feeling sorta stupid lately."

Robert's words were carefully chosen as he was weary of Buck's reaction, and it showed in his face and body posture. "We're re-releasing the old Diary albums in a best-of." The quiet and placid response from Buck built his confidence.

"You know, it could move, she's more popular now than . . . ever."

A conflicting ball of feelings began to fight for supremacy in Robert's bowels, and suppressing a surge of heartburn, he continued.

"I've been asked if you'd sing on a tribute album, some heavy hitters, big budget, major distribution."

Robert caught the beginning of a pitch, and stopped himself.

"Piper's gotten a lot of press and . . . uh . . . she's got a lot of fans."

Quite clearly Buck now perceived the permission, the blessing Robert sought, and he answered with a soft understanding.

"It's Ok, Robert. I mean, I'm just fine with that." Buck's statement was a calm, understated utterance.

"I think a tribute album sounds like a fine idea. We can give her end to a charity . . . or something."

The last word caught in his craw and tears balled into his eyes. Waves of unexpected emotion now hit him with some regularity, and Buck sat for a moment clearing his throat with a grind, composing himself. After a deep breath he eased the words out of his mouth.

"I . . . I . . . can't call her gone yet, Robert, I just cannot."

After a slight silence, Robert presented a disk from his top drawer, he carefully set it on the desk before Buck.

"This is the master recording to The Wild sessions . . . take it."

With a mounting of intent, Robert became still and direct. "Only you can tell me what is going to happen, Buck. Take your time, and you get back with me."

18

Enough became way too much, and Buck phoned a girlfriend who picked him up and took him out to a party in West Seattle.

When they entered the bash, the amount of intense attention was overwhelming. This strange new celebrity was akin to the regard he'd get at a show, but there was an undertow of something he couldn't quite bend his mind around. It made him think of Jacklyn Wright, and that thought drove him to the corner, watching life happen all around him.

The split-level townhouse was full of partying people. Everyone there knew Buck's name, his story, many knew his sister, some were fans of his band, others had seen him on the television. He was alone as he could be.

Slinking into the kitchen, he pocketed four beers into his jacket, two into his front shirt pockets, one in each of his back pockets, and opened the bottle in his hand. Out the back door, past a porch of smokers, he emptied the first beer, leaving the buzzing sound of the party behind him.

He walked and drank and drank and walked, and at about the fourth beer he started to sing. At beer five, it began to rain and he sang louder. Strolling east, under the freeway overpasses, past the industrial streets and the nighttime desertion of that section of town, he escaped the world, alone.

When his mind wanted to race he'd sing with more force. He just let it roll, every bit of it, and the cool, cool, rain drenched him to the bone. As he reached the I-5 side of Georgetown, he'd only two beers left.

Taking a right at Airport Way he headed south. Within a few moments, and without thinking a thought, he'd brought himself to Studio 420. As he rounded the corner, the sight of the building stopped his song, and the whole world came crushing back.

There was no way he was sleeping there tonight. As haunted as he'd ever felt, pursued by harsh reality, what had been Buck's joyful solitude now left him soaked, scared, and shaking. He saw Shwetty's truck backed in by the front door, and noticed the tailgate was left down.

Must be close to three, he figured, as he quietly closed the tailgate and canopy. Shwetty's home from his show, even lumped his gear in already. Could be more like three-thirty, four.

The thought somehow eased his mind. At least a part of life retained normalcy. Painted Nails had rocked some southend house tonight.

Smart money had Shwetty catching a forty-something cover band groupie and bringing her home. They were probably up there right now trying to remember each other's names and smoking some grass before the lights went out. The image released a deep chuckle that escaped despite Buck's ensuing depression.

He opened a back-pocket beer, and placed the remaining single in the front of his coat. After a deep drink he turned and walked north toward the sleeping city. When he reached Pioneer Square the rain let up, there was no more beer and the straggling ends of Seattle were calling it quits, only a couple cars drove by, even the bums seemed in slumber.

"So late it's almost early."

If anyone had been there to hear his slur they would have asked him to repeat himself. An instant need for hashbrowns saturated his body, and quickly he noticed the world was spinning slightly. He thought to head up to sixth for the twenty-four-hour, all-you-can-eat browns, but the bench by the tall totem pole called for him to take a break.

Once seated, he knew he was about to sleep, shutting down, everything becoming very, very fuzzy. As his feet pulled into his body, he scrunched into the bench. With his last bit of waking thought he reflected, from almost inside a dream, on all those times he'd picked Everett out of a bar, off some street, from a bench.

In a frantic start he sprang to his feet. An internal strength of will, a core demand for life, bolted energy into his body. He was at a full sprint in seconds.

Run like hell.

There was no turning back, there was nowhere to go but up. Uphill, and under I-5, up First Hill and faster, and move, and go, keep going. As he crested Capitol Hill, the pace slowed but his intent gained, his body complained, his chest heaved, his eyes watered, and he kept running.

He ran until he lost himself, literally. Somewhere deep in the Central District, he didn't so much come to a stop as he collapsed. Dragging himself off the main street and behind a building, he emptied everything from his stomach.

Within a minute he'd instructed his body to jog, and it did. Still desperate to move, his pace slowed, but his mind started to clear. Keep on moving.

Wanting to leave everything behind, his jog again turned into a relentless attempt at escape, and as he gained speed he just kept running. After traveling far further and faster on foot then he ever had in his life, he gradually became too spent to continue. In a stumbling stagger he finally surrendered, and his feet calmed to a walk.

The edges of the sky were just beginning to be threatened by the approaching sun and Buck figured he'd trudge some until it was late enough to call Bones's house. Mrs. Pine was the earliest riser he knew, she'd wake Jeff for him. She was so nice, and they were close enough friends, that normally he'd just ask her to come pick him up, but if there was anyone on this planet he wanted to talk to, it was Bones.

The early morning night was lit by the bright signs of the small and seedy store he'd found, proudly flashing its neon promises and promotions. Soon he felt too cold and alone to wait and he re-figured that it really wouldn't be such a big deal if he called right then. Leaning his forehead against the frigid edge of a payphone, his wet fingers dialed digits.

Exhaling deeply, he slumped back into the booth, letting the phone ring, and in three rings it was answered by Mrs. Pine. She wasn't awake, but her slightly groggy voice didn't sound the least bit upset. His breath was drawn in a stutter, he'd begun to feel very fragile.

"Hey there, it's Buck."

Her tone instantly filled with concern, and he answered a barrage of maternal questions with his soft and reassuring voice. Gradually he convinced her that all was well. Of course she'd wake up Jeff, who came to the phone with a blurry grumble.

"Bones, come pick me up."

Buck looked around for something recognizable. "I'm in Rainer Beach . . . I think."

Sitting balled against the wall of the still-closed store, his arms wrapped around his knees, Buck was a stone, staring into space. He wasn't asleep, or awake, nothing was normal, he'd fallen into a fog filled trance, a place so very far away. Only the slow cloud of his breath gave way to movement.

Bones could be heard a mile away, an auditory medley of muffled hard rock and his bored out three-fifty, but Buck registered nothing. Screeching to a stop, Bones threw his door open, walked around the car, and stood silently above Buck, who didn't respond in any way. A lengthy pause was permeated only by the sounds of the running engine, the muffled music, and the soft drizzle that had begun to fill the air.

It was a most awkward moment. Bones didn't know to sit, stand, say something, or not. In the end he simply extended his hand to his friend and held it there, patiently awaiting a response.

Neither Bones's hand nor his intensity wavered. He stood and waited. Soon Buck became aware of his presence, sluggishly he saw, slowly he smiled.

It was an expression of recognition, but it was also an admission of defeat, a beaten cry for help, a numbed stab at feeling. At last his right arm unwound itself and with a great effort he reached out. Quickly he was pulled to his feet and into Bones's angular embrace.

On the freeway, driving back into the burbs, it was all music and weed. Looking out over the hood of the Chevy was as much a comfort as the fat bowl in his hand and the pounding melody of the tune cranked on Bone's system. Buck felt as at home as he had since this whole thing started happening, the grass, Bones, and the song that strained the speakers were all among his oldest and best friends and for a moment everything was fine.

Hitting the long wood pipe with another blast, he quickly lowered his hands out of view. With a lidded snort Buck held the smoke until it demanded an explosive and hacking release. His body gave up telling him about exhaustion and a lethargic sleepy drone started to be replaced by the crisp bake and bite of the high-grade.

Eyes fixed on the road, Bones reached for the pipe, gesturing for Buck to grab the wheel. Buck drove with his left hand from the passenger seat as Bones took his quick pull. Taking the pipe back, Buck hit it again and decided it was dust, so he cashed the bowl into the ashtray.

Buck brought a rush of air deep into his lungs, the way singers do. Slowly releasing his breath in a measured flow, a calming, he then leaned forward to turn off the radio. Good and high, his mind had really begun to kick it into gear, and he could see, was ready for, the truth.

"Skyler is dead, there was a body, he's been cremated."

His voice was cold and without character, Buck had simply stated the facts.

"You know that television show organized some volunteers into a search party, big part of the follow-up show."

Bones started to speak, then listened instead.

"I know you know that. I know you told them off, and that you wouldn't even interview."

Producing a smoke without looking, Bones was fixed by the gravity of the discussion.

"Thanks."

Plucking the smoke from Bones's mouth, Buck gave it a light.

"I mean that, I really do."

He let the sincerity of his words sit, and then with a slight drag, held the lit smoke before him, struck with the sight of the glowing cherry.

"Everett calls it a parade, part of me thinks he's right."

For a second more his eyes squinted at the cigarette's fire, before handing it back to Bones.

"But I'm driving over there next week to march in their parade, and search for a body."

As the Chevelle found its way off the freeway and into the residential streets of the south-end, Bones declared he was going too. He'd drive. It was with the conviction of a pledge, some overstated oath, that he vowed this.

The sentiment wasn't lost on Buck, and just the offer made things less foreign and foreboding. He also knew Bones meant it, probably already planning the trip as he drove. But none of this was easy on anyone involved, none of it, and Buck felt it just wasn't Bones's dance.

While Bones had liked Piper and most certainly been impressed and inspired by her personage, she'd always remained an enigmatic figure to him. Only in the music had they really connected. It was Skyler that had become a brother and the loss had devastated Bones.

He believed it was enough hard times for his friend. Buck wanted to be at a beginning, to live again, but this was nothing he could presently afford himself, so he decided to cut Bones free. It was a physically difficult thing to do, a great will wrestled the vowels, the consonants, from his mouth.

"I think I'm going to do this alone, Bones."

They bought some bagels and orange juice and drove around until it was after six. Then they switched to beer. After a long discourse that walked the line of an argument, Bones finally conceded that he was staying behind, and Buck further grasped the fact that he was really going.

19

"No more Mondays."

It was with a boast that Everett made his declaration directly into the phone.

"You heard the news, already?"

Sharply enwrapped in Frank's version of the story Everett dropped some fresh ice into his glass and filled the rest from his current bottle.

"What? . . . Last week?"

A hateful rage sprung from the deep well of Everett's embittered resentment. Clenching his jaw in anger, he ground his teeth, and swallowed a good portion of his drink. His interjection was sharp and unfriendly, almost accusatory.

"You were coming back from the Caboose?"

Most every detail Frank had on the chronicle of Everett's dismissal from employment was obviously erroneous and inaccurate. Everett would have launched into an explanation of the actualities right then, if he wasn't still attempting to gather all the information he could. Still, single line statements of fact slipped out, only when they were absolutely necessary to illuminate.

"Contracts that carry the company, Frank."

For the next bit, he really stepped on his lip and drank and listened. Each word, every distortion of Everett's professional behavior, the supposed ill accounts of his performance, ate at him like acid. All these people smiling right in his face, stabbing him right in his back.

As Frank wrapped up the official story, Everett had half convinced himself that he was going to take the company to court, file some sort of suit. That idea made his mind become more realistic and he began to make a list of the people who'd soon be punished by the real justice he'd deal, his way. He left the thought alone when Frank finished with the first part of his report, and started on the second.

Emptying his glass, Everett absently rummaged for a cigarette and began slamming things around, looking for a light. Finally he pushed down the lever to the toaster and waited for it to heat up. Frank's last bit of new news changed the whole tone of the conversation and Everett slowly puffed his smoke to life as he raised his face from the heat of the toaster elements.

"Well, how many more Mondays you think you got, Frank?"

A meeting was scheduled for big Frank to talk to Bobby Houser at the end of the week and Frank's narration turned far more negative when he finally landed on this, the pressing reason of his distress. It was quite clear to both men that the realistic prognosis was not positive in regard to Frank and his continued professional prospects. The early morning liquor had worked its will with Everett, and his emotions were starting to play like a pinball machine, all his anger had turned dully sullen.

"I see, alright then, Frank, well, I guess, that's just what is." Accepting he wasn't going to do anything to anybody, that there was really nothing to be done, Everett began to tire, and became thankful he'd escaped employment as well as he did.

The rest were all just words, he listened to Frank's summation and speculation as he looked for a fresh bottle. It was an easy thirty minutes until Frank ran out of steam and Everett couldn't hear anymore. "So what."

There wasn't the rising intonation of a question, no demand for any answer, just a flat statement, a blunt attempt at blanket defense from the constant onslaught of accusations he was continually suffering. It was the pounding pursuit of placing blame. Everett was the only one in the room.

In fact, besides occasionally answering the phone out of habit, ordering a drink, or asking for cigarettes, he hadn't talked to anyone in whatever amount of time it'd been, he'd lost track of the days, they could easily be turning into weeks. His recent verbal bout with Frank had gone on long enough that his voice was raw, cracked, and hurt when he used it. Only the slight sting of the booze gave temporary relief to his throat.

As he pulled a long measured drink from the bottle, it extracted an exacting payment equal to every drop, dehydrating him of what little Everett there was left. He knew what it looked like for a man to drink himself to death, as he'd watched his father set the standard. Now he was learning the process first hand, and he could feel himself passing further away everyday, with every drink.

These kids. Think he was a bastard? They'd never known their grandfather, never met the old goat, never even seen a real bastard.

After an initial scowl, and the quick padding of a stout pull from the bottle, a smile eased onto his face as he thought about his father, about the old goat. The amount of hate he felt for the goat was only matched by the strength of the love he still held for him. Strange someone dead so long could affect him so strongly today, and with just a thought, like the old man had grown after he'd died, as if, with time, he'd become larger than the life he'd led.

Everett knew that he'd passed the legacy on to his own family, that in fact, he had expanded on it, dramatically. This sour pit of regret was the main source of his pain, a place he'd never known how to respond to. Unmanaged and erratic reactions spun a spiral that could only take him deeper into his dysfunction.

He'd known it was happening the whole time. Knew exactly what he was doing, could read it on the faces of his children. Everett always had to fight his father inside himself, and in his youth he'd done one hell of a job.

Made something of himself, become somebody from nothing, a manifestation of his own fantasy. The wild life he'd lived flashed through his mind. The places and people, the life he'd built, the music he'd made, his music, his life, his wife, and that is where he demanded it stop.

Everett reached for the near finished bottle sitting in front of him and made it empty. He wasn't going to places he should not let himself go. Not into those memories, not now.

Skip to the present, to this kitchen and another bottle, to this lonely little drunk, an unemployed, downhill, could-have-been cowboy. These thoughts didn't help his disposition. They fell like lead on his mind, and brought him to his freshest wound, to his daughter.

How? There was just no way that this was what it was, no way. Piper was a survivor, an ardent soul, she was nobody's victim, never. It just couldn't be, and he knew it was.

Affecting a rigid military posture, he walked on down the hall, from the front room to Piper's bedroom. He reached out and slowly opened the door with an aged creak. A few streams of dirty sun pummeled through the ratty curtains and illuminated the small space in a stained yellow light that revealed a tiny room, a storage locker full of boxes. Traces of the little girl who grew up here were mixed amongst the cardboard and milk crates. A blend of the various mementos,

pictures, stacks of magazines, boxes of guitar cords and
collected gear created a collage of Piper's life.

It was stacked and stored so full there wasn't any floor
space left, just a narrow hallway amongst the stuff that led to
the window. What does one do with all this? Everett walked
into the room.

Leave it all like some tombstone? Give it all away? When
Grace had passed that's what he'd done, gave it all away, get it
away, and many times since, he'd thought about all her things
out there somewhere.

Another time, deal with it later. That was the quick and
standard answer Everett gave to most every proposed question,
or action, these days. Think about it, do it, later.

Standing in the center of the room, he gave the mass
of clutter a good looking over. His eyes landed on an old
snapshot, pinned to the windowsill. It was of a very young
Piper, wearing a little red cowboy hat with white piping,
bearing an impish grin as she cradled a toy guitar.

Like an emotional magnet the picture pulled at him and
he staggered to it. Too precious to touch, or dare to disturb, he
squinted his eyes and pressed his face close to the shot. It was
easy for Everett to remember the day that picture was taken,
that exact moment.

So far from now, as far away as she is.

He turned to leave the room. An envelope deliberately
fell to the floor right in front of him. It leapt of its own will
from the top of a box, blocking his path.

As drunk and disturbed as he was, he felt no draft, saw
no sensible or sober reason for it to have fallen in such an
obvious and seemingly defiant manner. Stalling at the sight
of it on the floor, he bent down and retrieved the tattered
envelope. It contained a worn document, a single page that'd
obviously been unfolded and refolded many times.

It was the same documentation Piper herself re-read and obsessed on, a page clearly conveying the fact of her recent pregnancy. Everett read it twice then put it back in the box it had jumped from. As his body began to digest the implications, he was struck with a distinct sound that startled him.

A familiar voice, he cocked his head as he heard it again.

As soft and muffled as the sound was, it was recognizable anywhere. He knew exactly what he was hearing instantly.

Scrambling down the hallway to the small closet off the kitchen, Everett grabbed his shotgun. Checking to make sure it was loaded, he stopped and listened. Again he heard it, slow chords of music continuing to play, apparently coming from the detached garage.

Exiting the house, he scrambled across the yard toward the music. His breath heaved in bewilderment, and weaving slightly, the shotgun leveled at his waist, he looked around for a car in the driveway, or any sign of a broken entry into the garage. The single guitar grew louder, playing just on the other side of the door.

It stalled Everett as he thought he recognized the tune, something The Wild played, that rhyme, the one Piper sang as a little girl. Buck was on his way east over the mountains, could be that Bones, that was all he could think. Maybe some fan or something, whoever it was, they had no invitation here.

Everett landed his foot near the doorknob, ripping the screws out of the small hasp and padlock that kept it closed. Daylight was the first to flash into the open door, followed by shouts, the shotgun, and then Everett. If there had been a person making a move for the window, or a weapon, he would've dropped them, might have even asked some questions, only after they were laying in a pool of their own blood.

But there wasn't anything, nobody. Nobody was playing the guitar, there wasn't anyone at all, just a quiet and deserted detached garage full of rock gear. The guitar sat square in the center of the room, showcased in the streaming light from the open door.

Everett flicked on the overhead and hollered some more threats. There was no one. He was sure of what he'd heard, absolutely positive.

As much as he'd ever drunk, he was never this delusional, not like this. What . . . what the hell? Everett was seriously stunned, he started questioning his sanity, staring at what had to be the origin of the music.

Still as the room around it, the guitar was where it had been lovingly left by Buck, in its stand. The custom leather strap was draped over the back just as if Piper had placed it there herself. It sat in stasis, in silence.

20

Here, right here, this exact spot.

A catering truck, serving a line of people, sat with a trailer on either side. There was a large RV and a big canopy tent with tables and chairs all set up beside the deserted stretch of road. From the outside eye, the movement, hustle and bustle of the location shoot looked to be anything from the filming of a potato chip commercial, to the taping of a weekly melodrama.

But from his idling Mustang, Buck knew too well what the fuss was all about and he could discern an assortment of the activity, small groups of people were converging, speaking, pairing off, preparing for a search. He was over an hour late as his wreck kept overheating. But he was there.

Buck slowly scanned all around. What a beautifully desolate place, rolling hills, parched earth, ground-covering brush. Right there the road became more steeped in its slow descent to the tiny town of Vantage, and the Columbia river.

His whole life, he'd driven by this spot. Countless times had he passed right by and never known exactly where that actually was. Every time they went to a concert at the gorge, gone fishing, went to the lakes and the cliffs, were sent to see their second cousins in Spokane, all the years of going east in every season, they'd driven right by this exact spot.

Easing his Mustang down the slight grade, Buck was careful not to park next to a police car. He came to rest in front of the trailers, a ways away from the action, far from the canopy tent, and well off the road. Shutting the car down he changed to the fresh white button-down shirt he'd hung on the little hook behind him.

Checking his look in the mirror, he brushed at his teeth with his index finger, then spit on his hands to slick down the sides of his hair. He used his filthy tee-shirt to wipe his hands and clear the muck from the corners of his mouth. With two sprays from a knock-off cologne, he rolled up the window, grabbing a water bottle and a cell-phone.

The phone was one of those pre-paid minute deals, part of Everett's slim contribution to the campaign. Buck never worked so hard in his life. It wasn't just the amount of activity, all the stuff he'd gotten done in the last week, but the fact that he had to direct the action, and stay clear while doing it all.

Cleaning her house up, he'd gathered Piper's important papers, many of her most private belongings, and moved them to her old room at Everett's house. With Piper missing, Buzz picked up the mortgage on her house, staying there most nights. It seemed a sad little structure and the cheery warmth it exuded when Piper had lived there was gone.

With Bones and Shwetty's help, Buck cleared out Studio 420, loading most of the gear back to the garage. Tying up other loose ends, accounts, sorting and returning mail, even a meeting with an attorney friend of Robert's to protect Piper's rights and residuals, Buck just kept crossing things off his list. He'd gone so far as to do her laundry and pack the clothes into boxes.

Everything still seemed unreal. But when he lifted his head, the week was up, and his flurry of activity was finished.

He'd determinedly done it all without thinking too deeply about what it all meant.

The entire effort was to bring him to this moment, right here, now. Buck figured he might someday be part of a production like this, but he envisioned a video shoot, something musical, maybe a movie. Now he was a prop in someone else's show, albeit a program of great personal investment and consequence.

'Welcome Home' was positive, pro-active, community minded programming involving true stories and heightened drama, and was primarily entertainment. A very highly rated show, it helped find hundreds of missing Americans. It was Buck's best shot.

It made him feel like a wounded fish in the really big bowl, this week's sacrificial body, split on the altar of television, to the thrill of an unseen audience, fixating on his pain with their electric eyes. The notion left him with a mass of unidentified feelings. But he could decipher a gnawing need to gain control, define himself outside of this pageant.

Stopping behind the tent, he dialed up home and listened for the ring. Losing the call on the second ring, beep, and silence, he dialed again. In between the stutters of a horrible connection he could just make out Everett's voice, so he jammed his finger in his ear and pushed the phone tightly to his head.

"Hi there, can you hear me?"

Agitated by the fractured response from the other side of the phone, he began to walk slowly around, looking for reception.

"Hello? . . . It's me."

A truck barreled down the highway, making it impossible for Buck to communicate until it passed.

"Hello, can you hear me?"

He attempted to listen but the phone kept cutting out. "Today's the search."

Cupping the phone as he pressed it harder to his ear, he put his head down to listen.

"Did you hear me? Dad . . . Dad?"

Lost his link to Everett, no surprise there, so very appropriate. Buck told the lady at the register the phone probably wouldn't work where he was going, despite her company's promises. But it didn't matter whether it was on a phone with a poor connection, or standing right in front of him in person, it had become exceedingly difficult to command Everett's attention for any amount of time, impossible to catch him sober.

It was only a few short paces from the slim shadow behind the tent to the main stream of action. When he walked up to Jacklyn Wright, she was directing her crew and calling shots. As she continued to speak, her right hand landed gently on his shoulder, holding him in a polite pause, until she finished with her current business.

She certainly was a celebrity, a foremost example of a modern woman in action. Polished poise, she was forceful and stately, yet forever feminine. It was perfect, the way she delegated and decided.

Most every member of her crew had been part of the team for years. She fostered a family environment, while remaining the undisputed matriarch. Burying all the early producers, as any impute was deemed an attempt at takeover, Jacklyn Wright felt solely responsible for the success of 'Welcome Home.'

Ugly looks told him the whole story, he was late, they'd started without him. It gave him a chuckle to be living up to their estimation, or to their lack thereof, and he waited patiently while the others took their instructions. With a slight squeeze to his shoulder, Jacklyn shortly turned her full attention to Buck, and greeted him as an old friend.

The second unit was collecting master shots of the location and footage of the search. Two Boy Scout troops, folks from the ranchers' association, a church group, community volunteers, and some paid extras fanned across the area, all beating the small dry bushes. These cinematic images were heightened by the beauty of the natural setting and stunningly shot surroundings.

In front of a small outcropping of sharp rock, Buck sat in his white shirt and dealt with Jacklyn's probing line. He dismissed Everett's absence as an unfortunate necessity due to health reasons, a fact he knew to be indisputably self-evident.

The interview took about an hour and he was asked several of the questions many times.

Lucid, calm and fluid, Buck spoke of never stopping the search, of an uncompromised faith in the fact that she might still be alive, that someone watching this show could know, might have seen, something, anything, that could lead them to Piper, to the truth. When they were finished, Buck was led to the catering truck. He was told he could have the chef cook him anything he wanted.

Only the discarded bones of some downer cow, years old, were found and photographed. The rest of the day dissolved into what would become an impressive visual montage. The search lasted until late afternoon when a large appreciation buffet was held.

As the last bit of daylight dipped behind the Cascades, the location was disassembled. Soon the tent and trailers were gone, as were most of the people. Only a large RV and a small milling of the crew remained, wrapping it up.

Buck was glued to the hood of his car. His eyes were rigidly set on the horizon where he'd watched the day slip behind the mountains, where he now studied the early evening moonlight. The watery shine slowly set in to ease the darkness.

His white shirt was soiled, unbuttoned and draped below his shoulders. He'd walked so much his feet now complained, as did most everything else. Slouched into his windshield, he used deep sighs and drifting melodies to ease his discomfort, to distract from the fact, from the fear, that he'd now have to figure out what to do next.

"I'll interview the trucker tomorrow, I expect to use it as a centerpiece of the segment."

Jacklyn's soft statement startled him. She stood silently for a moment, then leaned against the hood, placing her face into his fixed line of sight. She left an intimate and silky whisper in his ear.

"Stay tuned."

With a tender rub, her hand lightly trailed across his back, and she was gone. Jacklyn instructed her driver to double-time it back to the hotel, and the RV fired up with a blaze of light and a roar. Besides Buck, she was the last to leave the location.

He sat on the hood of his Mustang until he fell asleep. When he woke, hours had passed and the moon was high in the sky, providing a generous light that bathed the night. Buck rubbed his eyes awake and gradually realized where he was.

Startled by his environment, he was aware in a jolt, and the spooky creep of his surroundings began to crawl into his consciousness. This place, and here he was, this late, and alone. Standing up from the hood, in brave defiance and with intention to face fear, he walked to the spot where they told him Skyler's body had been found.

It wasn't far from the edge of the road, just past the shoulder, hidden by a thin curtain of small bristly bushes. To Skyler's immediate right, that's where the guitar had been recovered. This was the last spot she must have been, right here.

Piper would never have left, not her guitar, not Skyler, not ever. In the core of himself, he decided she was most probably dead. With a calm clarity he further realized that the possible alternatives to that probable truth were a whole lot worse for his sister than death, and he wished she'd been found in the search.

Suddenly his focus fixated on a distant and muffled cry. It was an almost human shriek, a disquieting noise that demanded attention from somewhere in the dark. He darted to his driver's door and produced a flashlight from the glovebox.

Buck brought himself to the edge of the car, straining to hear. Again a just audible, strange scream filled the night. Easing himself into the dark, Buck followed his flashlight toward the sound of the bizarre cry.

His skin raised with small bumps. The noise was growing louder, when, without warning, there was no earth to walk on. Buck took a sudden fall off the edge of a sharp embankment, rolling down a long grade in a prolonged and violent tumble.

The extended whirl of movement ended abruptly as the light became still and Buck fell silent. The flashlight was dimmed from the fall, on its side several feet away, randomly shining into the dark. Buck wiggled his toes and cautiously moved every part of his body in a physical inventory.

After taking several readings he was surprised to find that, except for some dull complaints from a couple ribs, a few scratches down the arms, and a slight wrench to his back, he was fine. Grabbing for his light, he sat still for a moment. The sound was now such a shriek, and so close, it made him hesitant to stand, and so cautiously he came to his feet.

The screech reacted to his movement, it grew louder and more frenzied, blossoming to a howl. Drained and disoriented,

Buck took a step, stumbled a few paces, and then fell to the ground again. This time he'd tripped over the source of the screams.

It was a small lamb, caught in and bloodied by barbed wire. Buck highlighted the fleece with his flashlight, and it reacted to the light by raising the pitch of its scream and physically twisting against the restraining barbs. Its struggle spent the injured animal, and it moved out of fear, and began to bay, an exhausted plea.

From a crouch, Buck tenuously approached the creature. It pitched back in pain when he attempted to move a wire from the rat's nest that was its capture. Immediately he froze until it eased to a stop.

For a moment they were both just still, then suddenly it jerked in an impulse, attempting to writhe itself free. He leaned away to avoid being hit and saw the lamb further entomb itself in the wire. Its screams had the sound of a person, so disturbing a noise that it backed Buck off several paces, watching helplessly.

After a long struggle, it finally mellowed and he approached it again. Buck placed his hand on the lamb and it reacted to the touch with a small jerk. Finally relenting to his proximity, they rested together, and Buck attempted to heal the only way he knew how.

"Smile, child . . ."

Relaxing into the soothing timbre of his voice, the lamb submitted totally to his presence.

". . . prayer for the wild . . ."

The lamb became too still, and as it passed away the song fell silent. Buck stood slowly, extracting his hand from the expired animal, from the extinguished life. He raised his arm like it was a foreign object, and stared at the long deep scratches that raced from shoulder to wrist in smeared and running red lines.

His hand was bathed in the blood from wounds to his arm, and from touching the lamb. At length, and in a dazed curiosity, looking to the lamb and back, Buck studied his palm. Something he found there scared the hell out of him, and still holding his hand separate from himself, he steadily began moving away.

Dirty light from the failing flashlight lit the lamb as a light rain began to fall, creating a ruby gleam in the distorted shadow. The morbid sight unsettled what was the rest of his calm. Buck turned quickly, dropped his hands into fists, and gained distance in a scramble.

With manic movements, and after losing ground in a quick slide, he made his way back up the steep embankment. At the top, he gave a last glance behind, at the partially-lit figure, far in the distance below. With an audible gasp, he pivoted and ran frantically toward the road.

A truck could be heard far in the distance and Buck shifted to its presence as he ran. Bolting to the edge of the pavement, he strained his eyes to see the faint glare of the oncoming headlights. As it quickly approached, Buck paused for one second, relaxed into a comfortably numb stride, and steadily walked into the center of the road.

After a moment he mumbled the end of 'Smile Child,' and then repeated the refrain, and then again, each time with increased volume and defiant intensity. The sound of the approaching semi-truck underscored him as he reached a climatic screech and escalated his cry far past singing into a final scream.

His arms were raised in a V, his head and body reaching to the heavens, his figure was flooded with bright blinding light. The semi-truck's air-horn blared, drowning out Buck. Swinging his arms back, he bowed his body forward to meet the truck, and for a moment he knew he could be nothing but dead. "Anytime."

In a second everything was noise and confusion, a strobe of action, a suspended moment. There was a visual flash of the passing truck, locking up in a quick jolt, as it nearly jackknifed. The shrill screech of locking tires broke the air.

Suddenly stepping into the bright headlights was the face and figure, the unmistakable presence, of Piper Wild. She moved like lightning and instantly her back was toward the truck. Embracing Buck in a hug, she protected him in her arms from the impact, from any harm.

Regaining its footing and swerving slightly into the narrow shoulder, the speeding truck continued down the highway. Its horn blared angrily into the distance. All noise and movement left with it.

Buck was motionless, flat on his back in the middle of the road. The soft patter of the rain soaking the highway was the only sound. His eyes opened with a strain and he lifted his head.

Through the streamed blur and showering glimmer of the falling rain, Buck looked up in bewilderment at Piper, who stood placidly above him. In his amazement he attempted to sit up, but found he was weak and collapsed backward. A second before his head slammed to the pavement, Piper was there, catching him, kneeling with his head in her lap.

The last thing he saw, before closing his eyes and surrendering all effort to the depths of sleep, was her smile.

21

A wild animal, caged.

Catching the first wave of relief after what had been an exceptionally brutal storm of emotion and antics, he sat soaking in the anesthetized relief, the warm satisfied glow that comes after having lost complete control. His last refuge ended up being a small alcove in the kitchen. In the tightly boxed area, usually reserved for recyclables, Everett sat with his back against the wall.

As his breath eased from a pant, it occurred to him that he hadn't even thought about time since, whenever. With an encroaching feeling of isolation, he wondered what day of the week it was. The thought became a grinding worry and pushed a growing need for some kind of grounding, and that prompted him to glance in habit to the spot where the clock had always sat.

Only then, looking out across the small darkened home, did he realized the damage. A sick shellac of guilt, embarrassment, and disgust fell into his stomach, into the bowel of his being. Well, here we are again, big man, big tough guy, and what's the price this time?

With this last spin into infuriated rage, Everett had staged quite a brutal bout with himself. A major and prolonged drowning of booze had released all repression, and the eruption that followed destroyed everything in its path. He'd grabbed and smashed every dish, lamp, painting, table and chair; the entire contents of the front room and kitchen were reduced to rubble.

Then possessed with a methodic zeal, Everett had executed an obsessive whim. In some twisted need to dominate his own destruction, he'd gathered all the debris, every bit of broken property and discarded garbage, the entirety of his wreckage, and stacked it all into a pile, front room, center. All he could now gather from his dulled sensibilities, the thin residue of his memory, was that it had seemed like more than just a good idea at the time, it had been brilliant, a plan possessing great meaning, a mission.

As Everett gazed across the ruined home he knew that many of the things he cared about, irreplaceable mementos, and keepsakes, most everything he owned, was trashed. Yeah, that's right, he remembered, every little thing had gotten in his way, he couldn't see, or breathe, or find a way to feed his mind, his insides had ached and demanded action, satisfaction.

Nothing but a slave, to the drink, to the instant gratification of his rage, a foul tempered child, Everett was truly disgusted with himself. Sick with this behavior, he stewed until his stomach became a savage pit of angst. He could sit in his corner no longer.

Standing to a stumble, he found the countertop and steadied himself as he surveyed the damage. Well, this, this is the edge, too much, nothing but a drop to nowhere from here, never been, not this far. Everything was out of pocket, the present situation was abstract, and the glimpse, the distorted insight he received in his mind's eye, let him know he was as close to gone as he'd ever been.

Like he'd aged twenty years in a night, he felt broken. Everything, anything, for one moment in the sunshine, the warm and beauty of way back when, of way before. There was an assortment of smashed cigarettes on the counter, most scrunched beyond repair, just ripped up bits and pieces of what had been a pack or more.

Lighting the longest section he could find, Everett caught a glimpse of himself in the chromed side of the toaster. This can't go on, not like this, not this. The smell of the morning filled his lungs as he left the kitchen door open, walked along the slick porch, and down the slim path to the lake.

Take a swim, a cold jump into the water, maybe not come back. And what would the point be? So what?

Just then he heard it again, the chords and sound, the song, that guitar. How? Got to be in the mind, just demons, a subconscious reminder of loss, the delusions of a soaked and failing brain; there was nothing to listen to, nothing close to reality, nothing at all.

That was that. Laying flat on his stomach on the water's edge Everett dunked in his face; the lake felt extra frigid in contrast, his head a heated hangover, the water like ice. The stinging lake brought an alert awareness, a not so distant relative of sobriety, but still it was there, the music.

Maybe it was time to move. Sell out to the townhouses, to the pressboard, cookie-cutter homes that yearned to spring forth from his lakeside property. He was all set to make some nice money.

Then what? Go where? A chuckle leapt from him.

The main thing he wanted to do these days was be left alone. To sit, become as numb as possible, how pathetic and funny, who needs a lot of cash to do nothing? Just bar tabs and bottles.

Staring up at the house, he slicked his hair straight back. Excess water streamed down his face and shoulders, wetting his worn shirt. How grand a big fire would be, to cleanse, to hit a sort of reset, to definitively end and force a beginning.

Think about it, huh? Want to make some money, fire would do fine. Just then the music stopped.

Its absence disturbed him now more than when it played. Maybe there was a tape deck or something set on random, maybe someone was playing games, or maybe he was just losing it. Seemed he'd finally really isolated himself, completely, mission accomplished, such a marvel.

Run for the shadows, for any shelter, he wanted anything save this haunting. But where does one go? Home?

Leaving the morning sunshine and the whole world on the other side, he walked up the path, back inside, and shut the door. As his eyes adjusted to the dim pit, Everett deadened at the state of his house, irrefutable evidence that testified to the extreme extent of his own actions. Now it's dark, time to find some decision.

Got to get myself right out of here, go somewhere, do something, meet someone, anything to take the mind away from all this. A shower, shave, and thirty minutes later, here is a sane, together, semi-sober fella. Get a paper, see the sights, out and about, just any guy heading out on the town.

Emerging from the intact sanity of his bedroom to the sparse ruination of the front was difficult to get used to, but Everett took it in stride. Finding another broken length of cigarette on the counter, he rescued a chair from the pile of rubble. Placing it by the window, he hadn't sat for a second when he heard the distant ring of his bedroom phone.

Jumping up and hurdling a side section of the room's centerpiece pile of wreckage, Everett bolted for the call, ecstatic that the phone still rang, that he was on someone's list, alive and important enough to ring up. His answer was a bright and cheerful hello. The underpinnings of his voice still rasped.

"Frank, how the hell are ya?"

It couldn't have been someone better, it was Frank. Now we're back, back and at 'em, the terrible twosome ready to rip up the town, it's all up from here. Giddy like a kid, Everett agreed to meet Frank in one hour at the alley.

Starting the Cadillac with a repeated whine that finally choked into a low sputtering rumble, Everett stuck it in reverse and demanded the car react with a jerk as he stomped on the accelerator. Stab it and steer, of course he had to stop and get gas, and while he was at it picked up a deuce-deuce for the ride.

The twenty-two ounce bottle of malt inspired another quick stop at that little oriental place, the one that opens early and pours them stiff, used to be a donut shop.

One quick belt gave way to several others, and by the time he made it to the alley, Everett was an easy forty-five minutes late. Buzzing along pretty good, his perfectly happy frame of mind and positive disposition had found its way into full bloom. With every step he felt he was moving further forward towards the turning of some important page, a beginning as new as he wanted it to be.

With a glance to his wristwatch he saw how behind he was and knew it didn't matter, in fact it was perfect. With great volume and the most boisterous of manners, Frank would already be holding court inside, buying drinks for some louts he just met, burying himself deep in a pounder and calling for another round of shots; he'd probably ordered a mass of appetizers and had more on the way. Smart money said there was most definitely a lane reserved for them about an hour hence, so they could rip it up with the proper attitude, things were never better, just the way they should be.

"Everett."

The call came from the parking lot behind him and Everett turned, his hand on the front door of the alley, to see Frank, wearing a brightly colored flower-print short-sleeved shirt, short pants with a cuff, and a squashed pair of bright blue boat shoes. Consumed by a broad and beaming smile, the big man pointed proudly to the huge and shining motor-home he was standing in front of. The irregularity of the sight inspired a mumbled exclamation of wonder from Everett's lips.

"What the hell?"

Frank's short and stretched out argyle socks were at direct odds with the width of his tree trunk legs, and when, in a great bound, the ridiculous spectacle of a man crossed the lot, in a surprisingly quick sprint, the socks clung desperately above his thick, swollen ankles. He grabbed up Everett in a huge bear hug.

The size and strength of his squeeze, the impulsiveness of the action, caught Everett off guard and he could only react with a laugh, as Frank bellowed out his relief.

"Hot damn, Everett, we almost missed you!"

A sick sinking feeling quickly floated all the laughs and good times away as Everett got the word. With a grand gesture to the motor-home, and a most direct, sober, and excited sound, Frank rattled off what had happened, how quickly it had all been decided, just how fast Frank was moving, and how far way. Everett swallowed the shock of his sorrow, concealed his abandonment, and congratulated his friend on such great news.

"Well, let me buy you one for the road, Frank."

But they were on their way, in fact Frank had insisted on waiting another ten minutes, ten at a time, for the last hour. The motor-home roared to life with a double beep on the horn, as a silhouette of hair curlers and saucer-sized sunglasses waved from the passenger seat.

"If you see me getting smaller, I'm leaving."

Frank's departing line left a sad smile on Everett's face. But, hey, there was no hurry and no worries, everyone's got the right to disappear. He watched as Frank rambled across the lot, then merged away into traffic.

22

Blooming into a vivid blue, and adorned with a single white snowy cloud, the morning sky still retained a dark streak of lingering night about the horizon.

The sun was woken enough to cause a small steam to rise from the asphalt. Sprawled out on the side of the road, and sleeping like a stone, Buck felt the early warmth of the unfolding morning nudge him to consciousness. With a low growl and long stretch, he stirred further to approaching footsteps.

There was no time for anything to arrive in his mind, to remember the night, calculate his whereabouts, or gain any kind of composure. With a raw and alerted jolt, Buck peeled his eyes open. He blurred at the sight of a pair of cowboy boots, distinguishing the figure towering over him, from the bright dawn flooding into his skull.

"Are you still alive?" she said.

Touched with the intellectual hope of the eccentric, her rhythm was a quick quip.

"Did you see that? Man, what a sight, the whole sky, it was really early, kind of cold even, you know? I bet you do, what with your campsite. What is that about? Well, whatever, shouldn't even ask, your business."

A jagged slice of splendor, she was a sharpened beauty.

The boots, her lack of makeup, the denim and backpack all echoed a rural, if not country girl. But the quick edge of her wit, cracking caustically, spoke of someone seasoned, but with a defiant and cavalier quality that came from a combination of youth and confidence.

"People always got a reason for what they're doing, whatever that might be. You know you looked cold? Or worse . . ."

Items and ideas where introduced, investigated, and discarded rapidly, as she moved from one, to the next, interesting thing.

". . . but I could tell, I mean a guy like you, well, looks like you, a survivor, I can always see, it's a gift. I'm ready to accept that, know what I mean?"

It was fortunate that Buck would usually rather listen than talk, and that he always followed what was said to him.

"What's what, who is who, maybe not exactly, not all the time, but pretty close, a major percentage, I know, never tell me the odds, but when I let myself listen, there it is."

By the time they'd introduced, sized each other up, and started down the road, she'd told him more than he could have found out otherwise, about her, the bushes they were passing, the quality of the morning compared to the day before, and the day before that.

"Maybe not the exact address every time, but I'll nail that neighborhood, know what I mean?"

Nothing she said was vapid or unthinking, it was all very astute, informational even, but it was a lot, quite a lot, to listen to, let alone think about.

". . . and they are far more green than the other, if you really look. It's a silly notion to me, a favorite color. Name your favorite body part, right? Like I was saying, oh, look at that, when I was first . . ."

Her verbal barrage always gained ground when she was nervous. Any uncomfortable tension, if she was flustered, or feeling something she wasn't used to, the words came like turning on a tap. Already tense enough, getting a ride from some fella she found passed out on the side of the road, it was Buck's soft-spoken intensity, his interest and attention, the sincerity of his smile, the whole of his presence, that gave her both a measure of reassurance, and rendered the angst of a first date.

Buck got the impression that her mouth could only keep up with a portion of what was going on upstairs, as she broke many of her sentences into fractions, was constantly clarifying, and endlessly interrupting herself, clearly her chatter was a sort of social shield. But she was so enlivened as she spoke, so quick and cute, that he found it captivating, the soothing tone of her voice, she was easy to hear, and he smiled, laughed, and answered in all the appropriate places. There was nowhere to go but down the road, wherever, take a slow ride, and what would be better than to listen to this beautiful new friend, talking right to him?

Buck decided that every second of this morning would be sacred, the sunshine, the drive, the air he was breathing. The events of the night, of yesterday and last week, of the whole thing, rattled in the background of his brain. It had all instilled a feeling of fragility, of mortality.

He was still alive, relatively alright, and felt more like himself than he had in a long time, ready to rock. There was nothing to hold him to anything, just what served his immediate interest, no telling what might happen now, he could go anywhere, do whatever. He wanted to fill every moment with meaning, and that notion made him feel free.

Buck was as open to suggestion and invitation as he could be, and here was this girl, out of the blue, and that may mean something, right? And why not? He'd listen to everything she had to say.

She had assumed that he might, then asked if he minded, if she could burn one right there in the car. Buck's reaction to the offer of blazing up was so immediate as to betray the fact that he had left his bag at home. There were cops and dogs attending the search and he'd thought it best not to have brought so much as a single bud.

Now, she's got grass. How lucky could one guy get? Buck then remembered the context in which he was, where he was, and had to question the meaning of the word luck.

But here she was, and she was smooth, and gentle in her movements. Her body pressed against her taut tank top. Buck's veteran eye determined that her breasts were easily bigger than a B-cup, and nice.

A mane of long brown-black hair melted about the flesh of her dark tanned shoulders, framing a face that had a delicate, vaguely ethnic, bearing. The slender line of her torso tapered down to a tight toned waist, then expanded again into the ample and rolling curve of her hips. It was all in motion, every part of her.

Said she was born in Seattle, and had bounced between there and here her whole life. She talked lots about pictures, light, and paintings, declaring she was an artist, and held up a sketch pad to confirm the fact. Fitting snuggly into her large bag, the fat oversized pad was filled with drawings and doodles of places and faces.

Buck could see in a glance that she could draw, and did so, seemingly quite a bit. Could she possibly draw as much as she talked? The thought made him repress a laugh and when his mind returned from wandering, she was saying something about a mother who wasn't around anymore, and how her grandmother, who lived in a trailer, had taught her to paint, and what it meant to do it well.

". . . see that's exactly what it is, if you're not there at the moment, whenever, and of course wherever, that moment might be, then you miss it. It's just gone, or maybe never even was, as far as you, the proverbial you, or me, in this instance, is concerned. That's exactly the same as when I'm painting . . ."

There was a pause in her speech, as her attention was temporarily caught up rummaging though her backpack, attempting to find her stash. Even still, she mumbled to herself slightly as she was doing so. Her slight verbal lull was an opening for Buck to steer the conversation, to investigate. "Long walk."

The statement caught her off guard and she looked from her backpack to Buck with a stern and puzzled look.

"What?"

"That's a long walk to get all the way out here, August, right?

His question was like the re-starting of a great verbal engine, the one innocent squeak that starts an avalanche. "Yeah, August. Well, see that's what I've been saying, that's why I had to be out here this morning, time and place. You know that rest stop up from where you were sleeping? That is the last spot you can see the mountain from the highway, did you notice that? Oh, right, you made your own rest stop, didn't you? Well, hike up further and you can see more of it, the mountain, it's like a reminder, of elsewhere."

A soft sigh left her lips as her mind swept out stray thoughts about where she wanted to go, the things she wanted to do and be.

"But I try always to be where I am, I mean here I am, right now. I mean, we are, right?"

Be here now, that's what Buck had always said to himself, his own phrase.

He remembered exactly when he first heard the words of wisdom, he'd learned them in seventh grade from a large, grand and gray woman, Mrs. Stevenson, a veteran teacher who could spot a kid in Buck's circumstance in two seconds. Stevenson liked Buck and knew he was smarter than the average bear, just maybe worth the investment and effort, so she seized the singular formal one-on-one educational experience Buck had ever had, an after-school detention session where he was the only one to show. In that two hours of adult confidence, she said it a hundred ways, don't waste your youth, these are the best years, and so on, all of it, until she simply stated the phrase, be here now.

He connected to the idea. It was an applied philosophy the elder educator was attempting to convey. A visceral understanding of the value of time, he got it, and he'd held the phrase as a sacred charm ever since.

Who is this girl, to come so close to saying just that? And just now when he was saying it to himself. With a second thought, he figured it wasn't so rare.

It was all eastern or something, or universal, or what have you, and the way this August here ranted on and on she was bound to put all kinds of sentences together that might surprise one, in all sorts of ways. She sure had the idea, but with too many words. Buck decided to interrupt her with his valuable shortcut, he wasn't sure he'd ever said it out loud to anyone before.

"So what you mean is, like . . . be here now?"

"Exactly, who said that? Is that a saying? That, I'm sure is a saying, you know? Like that one, 'anywhere you go . . .'"

Finding her small stash box she thrust it up as a triumph.

". . . there you are.'"

As she opened the small decoratively carved wooden box, a pungent stink instantly filled the Mustang.

"Oh, now, that smells like home."

Opening the box, she revealed several joints and took one out. She slumped back into her seat and put her feet out the window. Pushing the cigarette lighter in, she licked the joint in preparation to light it.

"Now, if you're a lightweight you might want to take only a few hits, or let me drive."

The lighter popped out and August bowed her head below the dash, evading the wind. A large cloud of smoke preceded her arrival, but shortly she returned to sitting upright, holding a hit. As she passed the joint to Buck her voice was lidded and mumbled.

"Or whatever."

Across from an off-white dingy little lonely convenience store, on the far side of a hot dirt parking lot, backed into the shade of a tall and narrow row of trees, the Mustang doors were both wide open. The warmth of the midday and the weed left Buck fused into the passenger seat, singing along with the screaming radio. Thick black sunglasses, the unrelenting heat, and Buck's own involvement and volume, left him oblivious to August as she came up to the car with a half-rack under her arm, a single already cracked in her hand.

Once in the driver's seat, she offered a beer to Buck. Surprised that he continued to sing, unaware of her presence, she waved the beer squarely in front of the black sunglasses, and then held it there, waiting to be noticed. Nothing but song emanated from Buck.

She couldn't quite tell which was more amplified, which carried more, the radio, or Buck. Attempting to combat the volume and gain his attention was truly a joke and she let out a laugh. Completely amused by her inability to rouse him, she tried a full shout.

"Buck, hello . . . earth to Buck . . . do you want this beer? Hello?"

Finishing hers, and then opening the beer she'd offered to him, August gave him a listen as he continued to sing without notice. She took a deep drink, and offered it to him again, a quiet jest. When he didn't respond she drank again, and then spoke in the lowest of volumes, a private joke.

"Now, Buck, at this rate I wonder how much you're going to get."

Relaxing into the song until it was over she couldn't help but notice, this guy could sing, like sing, really well. Made him all that much more interesting, that much a mystery. She watched him sing, captivated by the passion and power of his sound, of his self.

Together with the wailing speakers, Buck and the radio finished the tune with a long and extra loud high note that sustained sharply until it closed. She turned the radio off with a click and a deafening silence replaced the song. After waiting what seemed an appropriate amount of time, August expected some response, greeting or salutation, but it was more silence, so she offered the bottle in her hand to Buck with a simple extension of her arm.

"Who are you?"

Turning the radio back on at a low volume, then with a slight tilt of his head, Buck slowly delivered a stoned glare over the top of his glasses.

"I told you my name."

"Yeah, Everett Wild Jr., or Buck, a dog's name, but I didn't ask you your names again, you know what I asked, tell me, just who the hell are you?"

She released the bottle into his hand and Buck took a long drink. He absently hummed along with the radio, finished his beer and opened another. It was a prolonged and stubborn pause, then abruptly with a burst of mirth-filled inspiration, he gave an answer.

"Yeah, that's what it is, I'm the singer, and when I'm really on, I'm the song."

"Well, that certainly clears things up. Explains what you were doing sleeping on the side of the road, doesn't it?"

He laughed at the question and answered with one of his own.

"What were you doing waking me up, in the middle of nowhere?"

"Caught an early ride out to sketch some of the morning, not near as eccentric as your apparent behavior mister side-of-the-road-sleeper, not even close to the same classification, not even."

She was right.

"I was . . . looking for somebody."

Finished again, he reached for another and after a cool swig, he attempted to slump further into his seat. He noticed again the increasing heat of the day, it was getting hot, and exhaustion began to really hit hard. With a deep breath that started at the small of his back and continued until his body had enough air to repeat the Constitution, Buck launched into it.

Without a break he recalled the entire tale, adding many relevant details, and without a note of digression. Conveyed comprehensively was the list of who, what, when and how; everything that had brought him to where he was now. It was when he got to why, that Buck quietly finished the half-rack.

August hit another blast of grass and fired up the Mustang. After a quick choke of coughing, she handed off the weed and stomped on the accelerator. With all the information she'd just been given, there was one thing for her to do, only one place she knew to go.

"Buck, there is someone I want you to meet."

Nestled between a public camping site and a main arterial, the tiny trailer park sat in a small patch of green, an

oasis in the otherwise naked landscape. Dotting the far side
of the area, at the foot of an impressively red and cragged cliff,
were a dozen or so trailers occupied by year-round residents.
There was fishing up the road and a store that sold mostly
beer, bait, and cigarettes.

Limping into the parking lot, the Mustang was
unmistakably tired. It was threatening to overheat and had
begun making a deep grinding sound that clearly signaled a
demand for rest. Shutting the passenger door behind him,
Buck patted the top of the hood, and sprinted the ten feet to
catch up with August, live and in progress.

". . . still the reality is that she's really all I have,
Grandma Ray, well, the only family, I mean. I'm what she's
got too, like her main connection to the rest of life, but there
is this wisdom, Ray is kinda crazy, that's what they said, a
shorthand summary, and old, I mean she is old, like old. Either
she is not sure of the date herself or it's some game, but she's
got to be . . ."

Walking like she talked, it was an effort to keep up with
her. The pace was much faster than Buck's usual gait, and the
beating heat wasn't making anything any easier. Struck with
another thought, she pivoted to Buck, handing him his car
keys and a question that she asked in earnest.

"Do you ever go to the public market?"

"The what?"

"Pike Place Market, do you ever go there?"

"Uh, sometimes, sure, got my name on a brick." "On
what?"

"On the ground, there's names on the tile, mine is
on one."

Buck's grandfather, the old goat, in rare celebration
had bought Everett, his wife Grace, and daughter Piper each
a brick before Buck was born, a campaign to raise funds for
the market, 'Your Name in Tile.' His name was the same as

Everett's, so he considered that brick every bit his, he'd earned at least that much.

Many times he stood on only his name, his spot. Knew right where it was, in front of that French restaurant, just past where they toss the fish for the tourists. Three bricks with their names on them, right next to each other forever.

"Why?"

"Why, what?"

"What about the market?"

"I love that place, someday I'll go there everyday."

That's not that big a dream, Buck thought, there it is, go. "Buck, I promised myself to stay around as long as my grandmother is . . . here, understand?" "Yeah, I do."

And he did. His arm slid around her shoulder and stopped them both. Lowering his lips to her ear, his breath warmed the words.

"When you're where you want to be, you look me up."
"You think so?"

"I think so. Make me a promise."

"A promise? . . . Sure . . . Why not? A promise, if I ever get out of here, and if I end up there, I'll look you up, get lucky with the rock star."

He answered with a smile, as she softly reached up and touched his face. Their eyes locked into each other, caught in the slow pull that becomes a kiss, when a loud and sudden bellow broke the moment. Each looked to see the source of a second shout, sounding more urgent then the first.

Her oxygen hose was at full reach and, attached to its tank inside, it was taught, suspended in the air, tethering her to the backside of the trailer. The one-time petite, whittled and withered elderly slip of woman, wearing a light blue, crumpled bed-coat, a long oxygen tube attached to her nose, solicited a cigarette from a large man in work clothes, and was now giving another ear-splitting warning to a small yapping dog, as it attempted to nip at her hem through the four-foot cyclone fence separating Ray's area from the next trailer over. Returning home with her pillaged smoke, the tube slacked as Ray looked up to notice August and Buck.

They reached the front of a dark blue single-wide with white trim, and a covered carport full of flowers.

"That's my grandma, Ray."

From across the way, her tone was made pleasant by an edge of willful humor.

"This one's mine, August girl, I grifted it fair and square."

23

"Too much salt?"

The interior of the trailer was cluttered, but very clean. "Got to season like hell anymore to taste a damn thing." Trinkets and paintings, ceramics, wooden carvings, antique sporting equipment, countless books, maps and mementos, memorabilia from the countless journeys and destinations of Ray's very long life were all collected and meticulously showcased about the trailer. Hundreds of faces, snapshots of family, friends and lovers, some black and white and obviously old, others in color, filled in every open space of the walls. August finished clearing the dishes and then set three teacups in the middle of the small tile-topped table, as Ray sat cozily in the corner chair next to the window and continued to muse out loud.

"I thought it was great."

Ray was the very silk of wisdom. Deep into an old age she never expected, she would often admit that if she'd known she was going to live so long, she might have exercised more and smoked less. As it was she'd been all around the world, chewed through four husbands, and a record number of cigarettes.

Part of that generation of women that first broke away from the petticoat and the powder puff, first introduced to real opportunity, she was done with husband number three by her early thirties. Left with two children and nothing else, she learned to dispatch for a large trucking company. She raised her children before society officially recognized that a single mother was something to be.

Her kids were grown by the time she married for the last time. She spent the remainder of her work life managing a string of truck stops. When she lost her fourth husband, a marriage of over thirty years, to an ugly illness, Ray sold her interest in the business, bought the trailer, and traveled whenever and wherever she pleased.

August was intent to tell Buck's story. She opened the subject bluntly with a quick synopsis, most of which was told in fractures, staccato facts, omitting unneeded sentences, losing all transitions, leaving suppositions unsaid, a physical and verbal shorthand entirely decipherable only by Ray. Sitting with them next to each other, it was easy to see the family resemblance, the dark, almost olive skin, the same shape of face and body, a certain consistency in their physical movements.

"Never met a girl named Piper before, knew a fella named Pally once."

Seemingly sporadic, she spoke in a manner close to August. The inner workings of her mind were as audible, but with less continual speech, her narration was more etched in her aged and animated expressions. When Ray switched subjects there was the distinct cadence of investigation, an underlying and methodical plod, a solid line of thought provided by her experienced and skilled curiosity.

"Closer I get to death more I think about what might happen."

Absently Ray drew a long cigarette she found in her pocket, and tapped it on the table, packing some escaping tobacco back into the loose and wrinkled paper.

"Grandma . . ."

Ray only really noticed the cigarette after it was lit, with its first full blast.

"I'll be damned, where did you come from?"

The deeply held smoke slowly escaped Ray's satisfied smile.

"Well, I got you now."

The tea kettle whistled with boiling water and August silenced the shrill sound, delivering a box of cookies with the tea. On her return she sat next to Buck, who had been listening as well as ever and was caught up answering a quick line of Ray's questions. Mostly answerable with a couple quick phrases, a yes or a no, Buck blurted the stats and facts of his life almost as fast as the queries came.

With a deep furrow to her wrinkled brow, Ray rested as quickly as she had started. Her eyes brightened, a clarity that only comes with an intense interest. She held a long stare with Buck, who neither blinked or looked away, his eyes as solid as hers.

Pouring herself a second cup of tea, August retrieved her backpack, produced her pad and a thick black pencil without an eraser. With her feet propped on Buck's leg, she began to sketch. Ray relaxed, slowly smoking, assimilating facts, re-checking answers, mulling and mumbling.

The heat of the day had dissipated into a cool evening and the last of a red sky bled through the light drape, infusing the room with a rosy glow. Buck sat as comfortably as he could ever remember. There was a certain warmth, a vitality, that radiated off both these women, a generosity.

"I was always a bit of a heathen myself. You a religious young man, Buck?"

"Gave it a try once."

The answer was a delight to Ray. "Once?"

"I was young, my sister wanted to sing in the choir. I was too little to sit in the sermon, so off to Sunday school. They held it in a trailer about half the size of this one, way behind the church."

Turning the page of her sketchbook, August paused from her work, and moved comfortably closer to Buck, who put his arm around her.

"I asked a lot of questions, and the big fat teacher hated me. Then I got in a fight with this big fat kid, they locked me in the back room."

"By yourself?"

"For a couple hours, I couldn't have been more than five. When Everett found out, he grabbed that preacher by the collar so hard damn near broke his neck."

As he finished, the memory brought him a smile, but it burst Ray into a radical laugher, a rare roar that hacked into a horrible fit of uncontrolled coughing. Leaping to her feet, August quickly returned with an inhaler and a glass of water. It took several minutes, but slowly Ray recovered her breath, and still amused by Buck's story, her voice cracked with a breathless mix of gravel and laugher.

"Sheep will always fear the maverick."

Sheep? Buck thought about what was a hundred years ago, last night. Swallowing the remainder of his usual shyness, Buck offered the story about the sheep he'd found, about its sound, and then silence, about wanting to give it all up, everything, about the oncoming truck, the appearance of his sister, how Piper had saved his life.

He wasn't afraid, there was no fear in his voice or body as he recounted the tale, just the facts as he remembered them. There wasn't the slightest hesitance to tell them. Only after he was done did he think how silly some might take his tale, or realize how seriously Ray and August took it, or notice the tears running down his cheeks.

The weight of the room had become enough for everyone to need a break and Buck excused himself to the bathroom. August closed up her pad, re-stoked the tea, and scooped a small dish of ice cream for each of them. Ray raised herself from her chair with some effort, untangling from her oxygen tube that was wrapping around her waist and grabbing at her foot, she then rummaged around the bottom bookshelf for several minutes, returning to her seat with a half smoked cigarette she found there.

August made her promise it was the last of the evening, so Ray lit it, dragged, extinguished it, and re-lit that cigarette more times than one would think feasible, as the three talked another hour away. When it was apparent that Ray was on her last legs, she started rounding it all in, refining and wrapping ideas in summary, like it had all been some scholastic lesson for her, as if she was their student.

"Buck. I've seen plenty go. I'm on my way myself." He held a need to hear what she had to say, the perspective age and earned wisdom allowed her. "Go ahead and scare me, Ray."

With a slap to his thigh she laughed, and then was intimidatingly still, her eyes glowed.

"Perhaps it's Piper herself that's not done here, huh?" That had the sting of truth, something indefinably solid about what she said. Every bit of Buck wanted Ray to help him resolve his indecision, to recover the peace he once took for granted. She saw his need for something served straight up.

The task of communicating always proved more effective when in the recipient's native tongue. Like speaking Spanish to a Mexican long-hauler. Ray chose and employed the two words she did, the way she did, because Buck had repeated them several times this evening, in different contexts.

"They will forever sell your sister's spirit, caught in her pictures and print, in her recordings."

Ray reached for the remaining stretch of her lingering cigarette, lighting the butt and exhaling slowly, her smoke mingled with the words.

"But spirit is like a smoke, burns from the soul . . ."

The subject brought with it a similar sensation to a scary movie.

". . . and the soul moves."

August reached for a brightly colored quilt and offered it to Ray, who declined with a slight gesture. The weight of the blanket felt good against Buck's back as did the warmth of August. Ray breathed deeply off the remains of her cigarette, claiming every last bit, as it was about to be too hot to handle, and she dropped the butt into her empty ice cream bowl.

"Buck, this much is very clear, you've got some serious choices coming."

24

"Maybe I ought to burn you."

The guitar sat still on its stand, inanimate. Just an abandoned instrument in a disheveled garage. Everett was perched on a folding chair he'd placed directly across from the Gretch, within an arm's reach.

"Burn you right into a pile of ashes."

Leaning close to the neck of the instrument, he whispered his venom-laced taunt.

"What do you think about that?"

His body was amped to grab, to bash, collect the broken bits, and burn. Had a lighter right in his pocket. It would never know how close it came to fire right that second.

He snatched the guitar by the neck and kicked open the case. Snapping the custom strap, his hands took over and with a methodic care he placed it into its case. Caught by the look and allure of the guitar, he held the lid partially open for a moment and then closed it slowly, the latches snapping shut.

Everett drank from a pint and continued conversing with the guitar case. It was upright and belted, sitting in the passenger seat right beside him. Parking in front of a music store, a large national chain with a huge sign hung on a cavernous building, Everett was winning the one-sided dialogue.

"I don't need the money you know."

He exchanged glares at the store's sign, and then back to the guitar, slowly blowing a blast of cigarette smoke at the case in contempt.

"Lot of times I needed cash, and you were safe." Unbuckling the case from the car seat, he confronted it directly.

"Gave you to my daughter, I trusted you, and what did we get back?"

With a nod of his head Everett knew what to do.

"Trouble."

Since he found unemployment, every sport-coat attempt at shirt and tie uniformity had been swapped for hooded sweatshirts and a string of worn sweaters. He'd taken to wearing his sleepwear in public, alternating between a dark blue pair that resembled some sweat pants, courtesy the double pipe stripes on the side, and the other one he wore today. Inches too long, bagged and wrinkled, bearing a faded green print with a long gray drawstring, they were obviously a pair of pajamas.

The case kept answering back, a quick retort for everything said. The debate continued all the way across the parking lot and to the door. He stood against the wall next to the ashtray finishing his cigarette and his series of points.

"Don't think I'll sell you?"

That was too much. To have his will tested in that way, his conviction called into question. He squashed the remainder of the smoke into the tray and turned to the store's entrance with a severe certitude.

"Come on in, it's time to show you what it is."

The florescent glare of the hyper-lit store stung his eyes and increased the queasy feeling floating through his body. Steering himself through the maze of signs, advertisements, and instruments, so many super special today-only deals, Everett became a little lost amongst the vast amount of product, and stopped in the middle of the store, a spot where several paths met. Increasingly aware of his inability to navigate whatever process was supposed to happen next, he was agitated, and quickly becoming irrationally irritable.

This was already taking way too much effort. A large sign declaring 'Customer Service' jumped from the rest and Everett headed over, taking his place in line behind a lanky red-haired teen. Why should it be made this difficult?

Everett hated lines, he hated waiting, for anything, he especially hated this. Some nasal tone punk whining about the mix he needed, about music, or whatever passed for it in his world, moaning about the equipment he was attempting to return, how it had failed him when creating his racket. With a voice like a cheese grater the kid complained to the clerk.

"Understand that I can sample that anyway, and at a live show it's all volume, I mean, for that kind of money."

The clerk bothered Everett as much as the customer. He was every inch the twerp and perhaps stuffed twice as full with himself. Offering some convoluted advice concerning wattage, he then consoled the customer by saying his band was having difficulty finding their sound as well.

"I bought this stuff from the head manager himself. When I buy some more gear I want to talk to him, what's his name?"

"Gary, he's here every Thursday for sure. Thanks, now come again."

The kid walked away so very satisfied, and then it was Everett's turn.

"You buy guitars?"

"Yes, sir, I think we still do." "You think, or you do?"

"You'll have to speak with our guitar expert, Chet. Wait one minute, sir."

The phone rang and the clerk answered it, gesturing to Everett for patience.

"Thank you for calling your music super store, this is Brian assistant customer service manager, how may I help you?"

Placing the guitar case on the counter with a loud impatient thump, Everett startled Brian, who reacted by stepping back from the counter and finishing his phone call without letting his eyes leave Everett.

"Yes, we do. We carry the complete series including accessories . . . . Pardon? . . . Tonight until eight, sir. Ok . . . thank you."

After hanging up the phone, the clerk now greeted Everett with some reservation.

"And how may I help you, sir?" "Guitars, do you buy guitars?" "Yes, sir, I think we still do." "Where."

Volume wasn't needed, Everett's voice was threatening just in its delivery. After taking a full reading of the man in front of him, Brian was just bright enough to curb his curt tongue. He politely pointed to the back of the store.

"At the back of the store, sir, in vintage."

Grabbing the phone, Brain pushed a button, using the in-store loudspeaker.

"Chet, used sale in Vintage please, used sale, Chet." "Chet?"

"He'll meet you in the back, sir, thank you."

The phone rang.

"Thank you for calling your music super store, this is Brian assistant customer service manager, how may I help you?"

A pudgy man in is his mid forties, Chet was holding on to the remainder of his hair in the form of a pathetically thin ponytail. He'd spent years in retail, done time at every mall in the area, and now he loved being at the music store, where he could wear a tee-shirt to work. Pre-warned by Brian, he was expecting Everett, and busted out his very best greeting and then his nicest letdown.

"Store policy is to offer half of our perceived value list price."

"You need to list a bigger price, Chet." "It's the buying guide I'm bound to, sir."

For someone who usually didn't speak of the past, a man who was never able to promote and proclaim as much as might have served him, it startled Everett himself when he declared his name, where'd he gotten the guitar, the song he'd written on it. His impromptu confession was ignited by the ridiculously low price Chet had offered for the guitar, an insult, but it was fueled by a buried pride, a rusted but living self-image.

"Yes, sir, and as a music buff I know the song, I love the song, but it's out of my hands."

"Well, then so is this guitar."

Suddenly the thought of selling the guitar, of parting with anything else he loved, of any loss at all, was unacceptable. Look at this, this punk, attempting to steal what he could never be, trying to buy what could never be sold. The thought left Everett snatching Chet by the collar with an abrupt and violent fist.

After a sustained moment of impending punishment, Everett could hear himself objecting in the back of his mind. Nothing was worth not leaving this store, getting out of here and back home, whole and out of trouble. This steady and prudent thought prevailed over his anger and slowly his hand relented, releasing the terrified guitar expert.

"Consider yourself a very lucky man, Chet."

25

August and Buck slept late into the afternoon.

With weeks in the past, their familiarity grew into a mutual understanding. That developed into actual intimacy. Neither of them had expected anything to feel so good.

Safe in the security of her small studio on the top floor of an old brick building, overlooking a gas station and part of the road, they camped in the throne of her queen sized bed constantly. She worked part-time at the local truck-stop, owned by an old friend of Ray's, and had hooked Buck up with an under the table, cash only, dishwashing gig. So from their early morning hikes when she sketched and he sang, to working in the evenings, to their late night beer runs, and the numerous hours of sleeping and living in bed, Buck and August spent an uncountable amount of time together.

Definitely she bore the brunt of verbosity, leaving nothing unsaid that she thought she might say. But Buck found her courage endearing, her willingness to tangle herself in her own thoughts. Engaged by her curiosity, and glued to her side, he found himself talking about things he'd never thought he'd thought about before, but must have, as he expressed informed opinions that agreed with and disputed her stance routinely, this surprised him.

Like a stomach digests food, the brain chews thought, silently, words only come as a conclusion, a confirmation of what is already understood. This was a reality Buck was living. So long had he lived in the quiet shadow of himself, expressing only with the prose he wrote in a song, and by the power and sound of his voice.

When pushed by August's presence to articulate, he was astonished at how many words were at his ready command and to learn of the conviction they carried. Sometimes the words sounded just like his sister. How Piper used to.

Tucked in together under the covers, she signaled a small television to life with a touch of the remote. A bag of microwaved popcorn filled the studio with a thick and heavy buttery smell, and stained their fingers a dirty yellow with each bite. Tonight was the first airing of the 'Welcome Home' follow-up segment on the disappearance of Piper Wild.

How do I not watch? How do I? What am I supposed to see?

These were all questions Buck had asked himself, and then August, constantly since he got the call concerning the air time. After mulling it over he made the decision to watch from the throne, only if she stayed strictly by his side, and only if they scored a bag of that really good grass she could get from the cook. August put down the sketch she was working on, loaded and passed the pipe, her hand landed on the inside of his thigh, an advertisement ended, and here it came.

"Welcome Home, I'm Jacklyn Wright."

Staged to be casual and cool, Jacklyn had dressed slightly down in jeans and a suede jacket. Hip, was the word the wardrobe department had used. She strolled a Seattle street in front of a small trendy café, her hands in her pockets, the tone and demeanor that of a classic television detective.

"'Welcome Home' encountered enormous response when we first aired 'The Piper Wild Story.'"

A condensed version of Piper's story was flashed in visuals as Jacklyn narrated the facts, and after her audience was reminded, the shot found Jacklyn leaning against the wall of a popular club in Belltown, a surviving venue Piper and everybody in town had played in the day.

"Our quest for the truth has been further driven by an ongoing demand for more and more information from you, the home audience."

The chopping thunder of a helicopter and a dramatic sweeping establishing shot of Eastern Washington along and around the Columbia River refined to footage of the search.

"So we did what we do, we went looking for her." Slick graphics gave transition to the footage from the location. Jacklyn stood arm in arm with Buck as both of them looked defiantly into the horizon. Buck seriously consulted his clipboard while speaking with assorted volunteers.

The Boy Scouts seemed to get most of the screen time. They pointed off in different directions, deploying around the area. All the visuals were tightly edited together and ended at the interview, staged in front of that small outcropping of sharp rock, Buck wearing that white shirt.

His presence on the screen was a slight shock to August, even though she knew the interview was to be shown. It just brought everything into uncomfortable focus, a reality that scared her. She shifted closer to Buck and slowly stroked her fingers through the back of his hair, mesmerized by the television.

"Well, Jacklyn, I don't think I'll ever stop the search, as she might still be alive."

How long ago was that? How would he ever know, unless he knew? Why did he wear that white shirt?

Racing, Buck's mind was on full tilt. His entire self was running around in uncoordinated circles rendering nothing decisive, and he thought for a moment he might get movement sickness sitting right there in the bed. In his time with August, and away from his life, he'd been able to pad his recent reality, and now the show had brought it all back, everything.

"I must say that even our Welcome Home team has been awed by your diligence, Buck."

Suffering through the rest of himself, Buck felt slightly better when Jacklyn, back in city suede and denim, stood before the large fountain in the middle of the Seattle Center and continued the show in the manner of a world-worn sleuth.

"After finishing this segment, Welcome Home received a phone call from a man named Earl Flood. Earl is a trucker who says he passed the location in question on that fateful night. His report bears witness to a struggle involving three people: two men, and one woman fitting the description of Piper Wild."

Dressed in a light brown leather bomber jacket, a breeze blew back her hair, just as the shot caught Jacklyn, greeting Earl driving his rig into the rest stop. They re-did the truck sequence several times as Earl looked clumsy in one shot and Jacklyn didn't like the light in another.

"Mr. Earl Flood, can you tell us what you saw?"

The interview was done in the cab of Earl's truck, Jacklyn sat in the passenger seat.

"Well, it's like I said. I was driving my route as usual and saw what I saw. A man assaulting another at the back of a parked van, a woman behind them, like she was flailing around, attempting to pull the one off the other."

Re-enactment footage was edited in, an abrupt visual of violent flashes corresponding to Earl's verbal description.

"Like I said, I filed my report with the dispatcher that night and left it to the proper authorities."

With its horn alarming the night, a truck blasted
down the highway. Its headlights quickly spotted the action
as it passed in a second. The blaring sound eased to the
background and the truck disappeared into dark as the cut
edited to Jacklyn, who stabbed with her question.

"You didn't stop?"

"Fight like that in the middle of the night on a long
stretch of highway can be a trap, any trucker knows that, I blew
my horn and kept moving."

"Earl, did they react to your horn?"

"Ma'am at that speed, in the dark, I'm lucky to have the
detail I do. It was long gone in a flash. I know it was a van,
that's what I saw, they were fighting behind a van."

"Thank you, Mr. Flood, for your time and cooperation."
She jumped from the semi and a tracking shot followed her to
the road's edge where she stood and faithfully peered down the
way for her close up, diligent and determined. A sappy musical
cover and a quick cut and next Jacklyn was on the upper deck
of a ferry boat. She delivered the big wrap-up speech in her hip
suede and denim, the Seattle skyline glistening behind her.

"Is it a real lead? This stirring possible eyewitness
account?

Did Earl Flood witness the murder of Skyler Ross?"

A grin had grown to a small chuckle, then an
exasperated chuckle had rounded into a roar. How could
he laugh? It seemed unthinkable, but that is what Buck was
doing, laughing his head off, and it made August exceedingly
uncomfortable.

"The smallest of details may be the key to this caper,
let's light up those phones America, and Welcome Piper Wild
Home."

He jumped up, got out of bed, and with some pants
and shoes on, the TV off, Buck had stopped laughing. He
stood there breathing in the doorway, his back to the room

and August. When he turned to her his face revealed how wounded he really was.

"I'm going to walk down to the store, get some beer."

She knew him well enough now to know that some air is what he needed. The smile he forced on his face said, I'll be back in a bit. Still, she couldn't help thinking she might never see him again.

The machine started with a blast of steam and a loud whoosh. Picking at the remainders of the meal sitting before him, he finished the abandoned fries and then sprayed the plate, tossing it along into the washer. Buck turned to his coffee, anxiously looking out the window.

The restaurant was doing a light business and the occasional roar of the semi-trucks outside punctuated the rattle of the diner and the muffled cry of the country music emanating from the lounge. August, dressed and working as a waitress, bussing her own tables, walked back into the kitchen to Buck with a stack of dirty plates. Putting them down on the long wet metal counter, August grabbed his arm and stopped him from spraying.

"He's here."

His eyes pinpointed a man entering the front door, recognizable from the Welcome Home segment. Buck watched Earl Flood, as he anxiously looked about and quickly made his way to the lounge. August grabbed his hand as Buck exited the kitchen, pulling him to her with a heated kiss.

"For luck."

The lounge was a dim dirty pit filled with smoke and a small gaggle of drunks. Two red faced regulars were glued to the bar, a young couple sat at a table nearby, and Earl was in a booth, toward the back, facing the entrance. The bartender spotted Buck as he entered and poured him a soft drink.

Accepting the cold drink, Buck greeted Earl with a smile. He immediately extinguished his freshly lit cigarette and softly gestured for Buck to go outside. On exiting the restaurant, Earl motioned for Buck to follow him past the parking lot to a series of semi-trucks in rows, some idled loudly, others sat dormant, a few roared past.

Right out of high school, he called a number from the classified ads and Earl Flood had a job driving a truck ever since. Supporting his wife and brand new baby boy was the most important thing, didn't matter where or how, long as it was legal. A fear of the law and any possibility of imprisonment had rattled Earl his entire life, the son of a perpetual con, he never wanted anything to do with lockdown.

Most kids from his neighborhood in Pontiac, Michigan, never made it much of anywhere without substantial damage of one variety or another. But soon came his twin daughters, another son, his mother-in-law moved in with them, and that's how life went. Of course he'd lost track of everybody from the hood, so it was difficult to be exactly sure, but he thought he might be the only one from his crew that made it this far.

He'd worked long-haul a long time until getting a plum job driving interstate deliveries. Still in love with his wife, he was blessed with four beautiful grandchildren, and fifty-one years of mileage. Earl Flood cautiously considered himself a fortunate man.

"Everett Wild, Jr.?"

Deep in the midst of the parked trucks, Buck caught up to Earl and started walking beside him. "Call me Buck."

"Keep walking, Buck, my name's Earl."

The two slowly strolled through the trucks.

"Yeah, Earl, I appreciate your interview with Welcome Home."

"Said just what I saw, told the truth."

In the shadow of the semis Earl suddenly stopped walking and confided in a hushed and urgent tone.

"Look, kid, what I know I saw, I'm going tell you, one time. Right now, and only you."

"Okay, Earl, shoot."

"I've lived here and driven truck for a long time now, hauling for a trucking company that's now owned by the Webb family, like a lot of things around here."

"Webb?"

"The Webbs, there's a pack of them, they don't do nothing but own."

Reaching for a cigarette, he paused to light it.

"None of them are nice fellas, but the youngest one, he's rotten."

"Yeah?"

"Rotten. Drives a distinct, custom van just like the one I saw that night, and I mean it. Exactly like the one I saw. Exactly."

Breaking to inhale, to look around, Earl's next statement was weighted with an intense gravity.

"You follow? Do you hear what I'm saying to you?"

"That's something I didn't hear about on television, Earl." Earl's reaction was immediate and defensive.

"A speeding trucker can't identify nothing doing eighty late at night."

The sound of a starting engine behind him made Earl react in evidence to how nervous he was.

"Guilty or not, he'd walk, that's guaranteed. That's the way it is. I'd be looking over my shoulder the rest of my life, understand?"

"What's his name?"

He handed Buck a photo of a well-groomed man in his mid-thirties.

"Madison, Madison Webb. Stays at a deluxe family cabin outside town. That's him."

Buck looked at the photo and then back to Earl.

"What I'm saying is the truth, I swear it, and I'm telling you because I believe it's your right. It's something I'd need to know."

There was a pause as Buck absorbed the impact, Earl turned to leave, then stopped.

"Want to know what I'd do? Just wish I could help . . ." Taking a step back, he finished speaking with his back turned to Buck, walking away into the trucks. ". . . but I never met you."

26

If Everett had heard the story Buck did, Madison would be dead.

He'd be just as dead as dead could be. There would have been no commentary, not one question asked. But Buck never even gave a thought to calling Everett, his mind was obsessed with what he should do, who he should be.

Driving a late-model, darkly-colored van with heavily smoked windows, Madison Webb was a mid-sized, scruffy and athletic, but attractive man. He had light brown, unkempt hair and dark eyes. Wearing a light blue sweatshirt and jeans, he was any average guy you might pass on the street.

Buck was lost in indecision. Still, he asked August to do some checking with a friend, got the license plate number and address, and then he had fired up the Mustang. They tracked Madison down early.

Watching him wind down the long driveway that led to his cabin, they followed Madison around the area the whole morning. He went to breakfast with a younger woman who was wearing a pea green jumpsuit and sported a mound of frizzled blond hair. Meeting what looked to be a crew of drywallers, he shot the breeze and gave instruction for at least an hour, then he stopped at the bank, and visited several private residences, soon it was early afternoon.

With no proof, nothing but the word of a supposed eyewitness, who had confessed to him in secret, there were few things Buck knew for sure, for fact. But this was the Madison that Earl had talked about, that much seemed sure. He looked like him, owned a van, lived in a remote cabin, that's him.

Where exactly does that lead? This guy looked like anybody having a day, doing all the things he does. Was it possible that this was really the man responsible?

Too many times had Buck had been told about Piper, someone swore they knew the real story, what had actually happened. Tips generated by 'Welcome Home' were in the thousands. She'd reportedly been living in several different campgrounds, abducted into cults, seen once on stage in Spokane, and so on.

He would have passed the issue by if it hadn't been for Earl, if he hadn't been so convincing, if his story hadn't had the ring of truth. A flimsy suspicion with no concrete grounds, no eyewitness to step forward and take the stand, was not enough to interest even Jacklyn, let alone any cop. There was nothing for sure, nothing that nailed Madison in place, that pointed Buck to an indisputable truth, except that as he watched Madison exiting from the store across the street, gassing up his van, there was a violent churning inside, a pure hate Buck had never felt before.

"What's to do?"

In the passenger seat, August was on edge, and even with a library ready to say, she hadn't spoken all that much, it was an uncharacteristic quiet, a rare restraint she was attempting to employ. She'd watched Buck become increasingly agitated with each passing second, seriously conflicted as to what was to be done about this Madison thing.

She wanted wise council, but Buck had sworn her to secrecy, and it was obvious that this was nothing to bother Ray and her failing health with. Taken to the hospital twice in the last month, she was released after a couple days each, but Ray's breath now came with even more effort, and that much less oxygen. Still, she knew her grandmother would speak of choice.

"What do you want to do?" "I don't know."

The pull of Buck's passion, the undercurrent of powerful emotion that played just beneath the usually placid demeanor, was what she found captivating, the depth of him. But this was difficult, an increasingly dark edge filling his look and words, and it scared her. She could hear the savage content of his thoughts.

"Did you believe Earl, what he said?" Buck answered without hesitation. "Yes."

Still focused on Madison, his eyes bore straight ahead. "What about you go to the cops, or that Welcome Home show?"

"With what? Tell them what?"

That was precisely what echoed at Buck over and again. What exactly could he tell someone that might be investigated, or even believed? Who would he tell if he did?

"Earl Flood never met me. Madison Webb is a fine upstanding citizen, from a rich family, and so on."

As the van pulled from the pump, and Madison merged away, Buck shut the heated Mustang down.

"Just ask Madison."

In silence they sat across the street from the gas station. The man perhaps knowledgeable, possibly responsible, drove away into the day. Tense to the point of rigidity, a tight chest and short breath, one tear away from a breakdown or blowup, Buck sat in a state of emotional suspension, just stunned.

"Let it go."

If there was anything someone could have said to confuse him more than he already was, that was it. Exactly what did she just say? He was sure he misunderstood her, the words didn't make any sense at all.

"What?"

"If you're so sure there is no way to nail him, then there is just one clear choice you have."

"What do you mean? Like, let him go? Forget about it?" "Or kill him . . . that's it."

His stillness was his response. "Isn't that it?"

She could no longer hold the tidal wave of her tongue.

"It seems to be the position you're in."

With a license built by investment and honesty, she bravely said what no one had had the veracity to state, not to Buck, not since any of this started.

"Your sister is, probably, most realistically, dead." Words are seldom so sharp.

"If she was anywhere, you would know where that is. That is no castle Madison is living in, there wasn't even a basement. Did you notice? No room to keep anyone anywhere. If she met up with him, if he is who this Earl says he is, she died that day. Her bones are in the desert, or she's some Jane Doe on a slab that you never found . . . I'm sorry."

Only with his eyes closed and a hand on his back, her breath beside him, could he hear what he'd heard, or say out loud what he said.

"I know."

"Who can you tell? Cops will call you crazy, or not have enough to go on when your friend Earl disappears, or perhaps they won't care because they're bought off, and find a way to bury what you do bring to their attention. Even if the authorities were supposedly on your side, look at that one Green River guy, killed more people than anyone ever, and even he got off, or lived anyway."

Buck remembered watching the TV with the rest of the Northwest as that beady eyed demon said guilty over and over, pure evil.

"And remember this Madison's got money. Really Buck, backed into this kind of corner, it seems clear you have a direct choice, you can either let it go, remember your sister with love, and live a life. Or, since there seems to be no other justice at hand, it is you, yourself . . . anything else creates a bigger mess than you have now, or could ever want."

Her pause was an attempt at remembering just the right words, something she had read.

"If the time comes in the time of your life to kill, kill and have no regret."

Then she reached for words of her own.

"But I think only you can decide if that time is right. It's your life. What do you want to live with?"

Buck heard every word she said to be the truth.

"Buck, whatever you decide, I would never say a thing, to anyone, ever."

He believed her. She would never betray him in any way. He trusted her opinion, the things she had to say, and the way she felt.

"So you're saying, that I either drop it, or I . . . kill him myself."

"And if you do that . . ."

August handed Buck the picture of Madison. ". . . who would you become?"

After the sun had fallen and they'd returned to her apartment, she sat rummaging through Buck's bag, holding different garments up, items for inspection, until, taking off her top, she put on the white button-up shirt from Buck's bag. He entered from the bathroom and shut the front curtains to the apartment. Freshly showered, with just a towel wrapped around his waist, Buck sat on the edge of the bed with a laugh, and then he saw that look in her eyes.

"What do you want to do tonight?"

She moved like a song, straddling him where he was. With a mischievous touch she surveyed his damp and naked body, playfully stroking through his hair. He reached his hand up to caress her face, then firmly cupped the back of her head, and they kissed.

They passed the night naked and entwined in a world of only two and shared a passion reserved for all life that is young, learning, and so very much alive. At daybreak they were still together. Way past dawn in the heat of the late morning, did they finally exhaust into the arms of sleep.

All day they rested in each other's embrace, and as the light was clocking into night the lethargic weight of Buck's eyes eased to life. He stayed just as still as he could be. Some sights Buck burnt into his mind, and his ability to record was never so stimulated as when he slowly surveyed this taught body of flesh, his entangled self with her, like this.

It'd been long enough now that it seemed that this is how life was, was supposed to be. These hot August nights, surreal. Like all ordinary life had been suspended in respect of something so much better.

Softly untangling himself, Buck rose from the bed and walked to the window. The splitting daylight illuminated his bare form against the light blue sheet pinned up as a curtain, and he looked out with a stretch, watching the day fade away. August's easel was placed by the window, and Buck accidentally gave it a knock as he reached out his arms wide.

Quickly catching a small painting before it fell to the floor, he was caught by its color. Usually when he looked at her art, she was chatting in his ear. He liked her work, but hadn't found the silence to look, to absorb, to hear the pictures.

After a long silent stare, studying the rendering of a sunrise, he decided it was good. Not only technically good, but it had a quality, a certain flair that made it cool, like everything she did it was elevated, heightened to something spiritual. Seemed she was developing an individual, singular voice, a distinctive manner and approach, a style.

Light is what she claimed to paint, even with just a pencil, but looking across the apartment he saw that she painted, drew, and doodled just about everything she could. In fact, besides the bed, the TV, the end-table and that old chair, the only things here were her pictures and drawings, a few framed, all tacked to the walls. You could clear the place out in no time.

Returning the unfinished sunrise to its spot, he noticed her sketch pad on the sill. He hadn't really taken a good look at it. Buck could tell it was something personal, not just intimate, but sacred to part of her process, private, like a diary.

After only a hint of deliberation, he gave her a good look to see if she was still asleep, and then started thumbing through pages. There were more doodles than anything else, lots of notes about color and line. Most of the sketches had squiggles, arrows and boxes, that had to be some form of shorthand intelligible to her alone.

What he hadn't seen, he'd recognized from its source. Like her depiction of that old sheepdog that hung around the café's garbage dumpster looking for food. She'd caught the canine's scrappy character and yet made him into more than he was, eloquently animated him, bestowed a life and timeless character, all with nothing but a number two pencil.

For her to be this good at something made him like her all that much more, excellence was something he'd always respected. Turning the next page revealed an exact sketch of Buck sitting next to Ray, it was so perfectly them, at the table in her trailer. When he looked at the next drawing, a startled shiver froze his hand.

It disturbed him, the detail, the shading and streams of the early morning light, how they hit the subject, this still young man laying next to a desolate highway, the twist in his hips, the angle of his feet. It was a snapshot rendering of Buck, that morning, right before she woke him, sleeping on the side of the road. He'd been her subject before they'd ever met.

Placing the pad down carefully, he crossed back to the bed where he stood and watched August breathe, the mystery that was her. Just his skin not being next to hers made him miss the soft flow of her body. He was addicted to the silk of her hair, the valley of her eyes, the sublime charge her presence provided.

Wishing he could live in this fold forever, of last night, of right now, Buck recognized the gnawing need to be somewhere else, to do whatever might need to be done. There was no way he could just forget what Earl had told him, to let anything go.

He had to take some action, and there was no way she should be involved, at all, not even as much as she was already, so, after a long moment, he sat gently on the bed and spoke very softly.

"I could, I think I do . . ."

Leaning his lips next her ear, his breath was the slightest whisper.

". . . love you."

It was the first time he had said that. Said it and meant it, meant it like this. Seldom had any word fallen so pathetically short of what he really wanted to say, or taken so much courage to give voice to.

"But, I've got to go."

Kissing her gently on the cheek the decision was sealed. It didn't take him two minutes to get his shoes and shirt on and grab his bag. After Buck was completely gone, the door was shut, and the tread of his steps disappeared down the stairwell, August opened her eyes, awake but resigned, and somehow she tried to smile.

"See you later, Buck."

Built on the edge of a high bluff, Madison's secluded cabin had large angled windows and a tall alpine roof. Buck looked down from his perch to the driveway of the house below him. From where he stood on his small brush-covered knoll above the home, the inside looked warm.

Hours he sat watching. His car was parked an easy five miles away, next to a row of other used vehicles all with 'for sale' signs on them. The number in the Mustang's window dialed to nowhere, he wouldn't sell his ride in reality, it was a nondescript place to park.

The entire day, and part of the next, Buck watched. He barely slept, when he did it was restless and laden with fits of panic and fear. It was the weekend and Madison was in and out several times, but mostly home. Anytime he went somewhere he drove that van.

The spinning turnstile his mind had become was making Buck sick to his empty stomach, and his stretched nerves had carried him well past any passion for further debate. The questions had just kept coming in for far too long, pushing thought to the place that it had no use, nothing decisive to render, just an endless maze of points and counter-points strung together in an incessant circle.

What was right and wrong, and how did it apply? What could he live with now, years from now? The repercussions of every angle haunted his thoughts until Buck could stand it no longer.

His legs were the first to rebel against this intellectual tyranny, to stand, to demand action. The rest of himself agreed it was time to do something and the roof chatter of his mind was forced to a backseat as he scaled down the hill toward

Madison's cabin. With no weapon, and not a thought of what he might say, Buck hadn't a plan at all.

Like a diver who'd just left the board, he was committed. It was all motion from here. But it was beyond his power not to stop at the van and peer into its smoked widows, impossible for him not to walk up to the cabin.

After only a tremor of hesitation, he knocked on the door. Then knocked again. Harder.

In only a moment, Madison opened the door dressed in jeans and polo shirt, close up he was better than average looking, but frayed, an aging frat boy smoking a thin sweet cigar. "Well, what can I do for you?"

"Hi . . . my car broke down at the end of your driveway, can I use your phone?"

"What are you doing out this way?" "I got lost."

"Yeah, you got lost alright, pal. Hold on."

He left the door half-open, and walked into the house, speaking back over his shoulder.

"How the hell you get lost out here? There's only two roads."

Inside the doorway, attached to the wall, within an arm's reach of Buck, there was a coat rack. To the left, next to a parka and scarf, was a long white leather jacket, and pinned to the lapel, a small pink peace sign. Many coats could match this one, the little pin was nothing special, just a button sold in any number of places.

But there was no doubt in Buck's mind that that particular pin on the collar of that exact jacket had belonged to his sister.

A couple of seconds, he had only a sliver of a moment to decide what to do. Part of him wanted to turn and run, to be anywhere but here, but his eyes couldn't leave that jacket, that pink pin. Bothered by the imposition, this kid, Madison approached abruptly with the phone.

"Call a tow truck, or whomever, and leave the phone on the porch here, Ok?"

"Sure."

As the door closed, Buck weighed his last alternatives, filing over the options in a split second, when his indecision lost out to his fist. With a kick he flung the door open, and a startled Madison turned to catch a punch to the throat. Without any hesitation Buck repeated the blow, striking an already gasping Madison in the neck again.

In anything close to a fair fight Madison would have more than an edge, he was older, thicker, and had a vast amount of experience when it came to violence. Buck had been in some brawls, most of those times he was drunk, but he in no way considered himself a fighter. He did, however, know enough not to stop now.

A series of punches stood unanswered as Madison lost his footing. He landed on the floor with a thump that couldn't have done his head any good. Then the kicks came, a bunch of them.

By the time Buck came to his first pause to breathe, it was already over. He had beaten him into submission. Madison was clutched to the ground, attempting to pull himself away from Buck, muttering broken words with a breathless whine.

That wasn't where Buck was going to leave it. With a renewed rage in his heart and Piper's jacket in his hand, Buck turned back to Madison, who'd barely made it to his first knee in an attempt to stand.

Buck took the couple of steps to shut the front door. Madison strained to get to his feet. Buck calmly watched him find the wall and slowly prop himself up, turning to face his assailant.

"Hi, I got a couple questions for you."

Thrusting the jacket toward Madison he demanded an answer.

"Where did you get this?"

Madison's answer was to spit, a bloody spray of defiance. Buck threw the jacket at Madison. It hit him in the chest, but before it fell to the floor Buck landed again.

In a manner close to an execution, Buck coldly cracked him with a flurry of fists, with his bare hands. Madison rolled backward, screaming in an ear-curdling pitch. A knuckle struck on the edge of his cheek, removing a swath of skin and the blood was suddenly everywhere.

Buck had gained momentum, allowing himself to feed on his own rage, to fuel it. He didn't really expect any answers. But the questions felt good to ask, each accompanied with more violence.

"Is that your van out front?"

Madison rolled in agony, grabbing at his chest, balling into in a bloody screaming heap.

"Answer me, is that your van?"

With great effort, and in hopes of not getting hit again Madison choked out his answer. "My . . . my van, yeah, it's mine."

Buck swung a blow that resonated with the sound of a snapping rip. Madison was a ball of broken pain, writhing next to the wall. Buck grabbed him up by the throat, his prey pleading like a dying animal.

"A couple, a man and woman . . . you . . . your van."

A look of deep horror filled Madison's face, Buck tightened the grip on his neck and burned into his eyes.

"You know what I'm talking about?" "I don't know, I . . . my . . ."

Madison tried to move, his body, his eyes, anything, but Buck found new anger in this attempt to deflect.

"You do. You know. You know what I'm talking about, and you are going to tell me, a man, a woman . . ."

With Madison's throat still in his hand, Buck delivered additional slaps to the face, each attended to with a question.

"You going to tell? Want to die? You know what I'm talking about?"

Madison was able to produce only a squeak of a word at a barely audible level. ". . . yeah . . ."

The answer was like a punch and he reeled away, releasing Madison. Struck with sudden inspiration, Buck became very calm, bent over and picked up the thin sweet cigar, still burning. Blowing on the cherry of the cigar, the tip glared red hot.

"You leave my friend Skyler dead on the street like a pile of garbage?"

Buck's voice was frigid.

"Did you?"

With a perverse intimacy he lowered his face next to Madison's.

"The girl, where is she? . . . Tell me."

Madison shook his head no, and closing his eyes, gasped to breathe. A pungent smell of cigar smoke filled the air as Buck blew on the fire. Then he began to slowly move the butt to the side of Madison's face, getting close enough to heat the skin.

"Here's what it is."

Madison's face twisted, his scream was muffled as Buck's hand closed around his mouth. He was a second away from a burnt and suffocating end, when Madison's suffering eased.

Buck's attention shifted to a figure standing beside them, watching.

It was Piper.

Squinting his eyes for confirmation, straining to understand, he couldn't deny the exact form and figure of his sister, Piper Wild. She softly looked to Buck, her gesture and presence questioning his present actions, the savage motion of his assault. In that moment, Buck observed himself, his intent, the cigar.

Everything he was wanted to end Madison, to end him. But looking at Madison and then back to Piper, he saw himself, in his mind's eye. Right then, Buck understood his life was worth more than any death.

Abruptly he ground the cigar on the wall behind Madison's face. Slowly releasing his hold, he stood and met Piper's eyes, it was her, but she was a long, long way away, here, yet somewhere else. Stunned, looking for understanding, he reached out, in a soft, confused voice.

"Piper?"

Her answer was easy.

"Good choice, go home, Buck . . . go."

The next second there was no cigar, no cabin, no screaming Madison. Buck was behind the wheel of his Mustang, driving up to August's place. The light blue sheet was gone, he could see right in, and a single bulb burning bright revealed the place to be empty.

He sped the Mustang about-face. In his head he replayed how many times August had told him why she was still here, how badly she needed to leave, to get out, to go, and that when Ray checked out, she would be gone later that day. The way he'd bolted away, so self involved, he hadn't left his number or address, all he had of her was her name, August Brooks.

Strange how well he knew these roads, how it was a place he'd grown accustomed to, and how different it suddenly seemed without August. As he peeled into the parking lot, he spotted two men carrying an oxygen tank out of Ray's trailer and he knew for sure. As a formality he stopped the car next to them.

"Excuse me, do either of you guys know Ray?"

The smaller of the two men answered Buck's question as they loaded the tank onto their truck.

"Sure, we knew old Ray."

"She was a kick in the head, that lady." "Was?"

"Yeah, don't you know, kid? She's gone."

27

Cackling under the small 'Cocktails' sign, deep in the arms of a dark and hairy Italian man, it was her laugh he remembered.

Red neon shed over the two-person spectacle. The woman, mostly concealed in his thick arms, mashed in a heave of drunken passion with the Italian, barring the entrance to Diamond Jack's. The sight was enough to have just turned a party of four, looking for a drink, to go somewhere else.

If Everett hadn't been a regular, he might not have been so apt to enter around the absurd obstacle. He was on his way to the lounge, and it wasn't until he passed them by that he caught a glimpse of her, and put that laugh to that face. It was the one that got taken away, it was April.

She was so obviously submerged into a blind drunk that her eyes bore no recognition, as she told Everett to take a picture, it would last longer. He just walked on by, into the lounge and found his stool. Sitting down in one of his favorite spots Everett was now sullenly dissatisfied.

It was near closing time and he had just woken up, day, night, something for someone else to worry about. It'd been a while since he'd fully dressed, a button up shirt, a jacket, shoes that didn't pull on. He thought it was a perfect time to see Del and drink 'til close.

But that sight in the doorway, her fading giggle as the Italian finally led them off into the dark of the parking lot, gave Everett's stomach a turn. Everything around him seemed cheap and shallow. Even Del looked like a sorry little man pathetically pushing lighter fluid in a windowless pit.

Two quick beers, a couple shots and he was gone, didn't even stay for closing. Out of his trunk came a bottle. Everett's growing disillusionment with this world left him in the mood to really drink, and drive.

When he was driving free, he had control. The accelerator, brakes, every left and right, all at his command, his whim. Nothing was ever out of his hands, not when he was driving, that only happens when you crash, and that's something you don't think about.

Wet pavement and hair-pin corners, it was the Cadillac and Everett against Redondo hill. The track was wet, and he had to pass some slug in a minivan at the top to get a clear run, but now it was all whirling hands and fishtails. Adrenaline fought alcohol for dominance and from somewhere deep in between, Everett let out a dark shout at the danger.

Every inch of the road was theirs, Everett and the Cadillac owned it, an incontrovertible fact, a new speed record was set, a personal best for them both. With the last of the steep winding incline behind, he slowed it down to cruising speed, clicked on the radio and eased it along the narrow stretch of waterfront. It was an easy crawl up the back roads to home, and a good thing, as Everett noticed he'd all but killed the bottle.

The headlights pierced the darkness and he navigated the winding tree-lined road. Shafts of moonlight intermittently illuminated the night, creating pockets of dark and clearings of visibility. Lighting a cigarette, Everett caught the sight of a figure in the distance.

To see, he wiped the inside of the window with his hand. A climbing terror knocked at his insides, something was wrong.

As he turned on the high-beams, looking intently, Everett discovered whatever he thought he'd seen wasn't there now.

In the background, the song on the radio had ended. Quickly came a station identification. It was complete with a choir singing the call letters and an extended harmony declaring, 'The best oldies of all time, all the time.'

The familiar chords of 'Touch of Grace' started to play and the sound of his own song startled him. Everett looked from the radio to the road, and his attention was caught again by the same figure. Just as the sight became clearly discernible, a young lady hitchhiking, she was gone.

Passing the bend where he saw her standing, he craned his head, slowing slightly. Disturbed by the song, he started to reach for the radio when abruptly, he was struck by the unmistakable sight of his daughter, of Piper. She was standing in the middle of the road, directly in the path of the speeding Cadillac.

Everett raised one arm to protect himself. The other arm swerved the car into a jackknife. After a long squeal, and a spin, the Cadillac slammed into a tree, bounced off and came to a screeching halt near the edge of the pavement.

Tossed around pretty good, it took Everett a few moments to assess his damage, and then grab a flashlight from the trunk. He inspected the Cadillac, its new dent and damage, and then the area. Looking all around, scanning the night with his flashlight he came to rest in the middle of the deserted road.

After a moment his hands and the light fell to his sides. The idling car and the chorus to 'Touch of Grace' playing on the radio broke the still, empty darkness. There was no one.

Not satisfied, he marched up a piece, and around the next curve. Emphatic to find Piper, or an answer, he almost tripped over a large branch laying on the road. He followed the limb with his eye to the downed tree it was connected to, blocking the street in deadly obstruction.

Good thing he'd stopped, hit this thing doing cruising speed it could be big trouble, could've been the end.

"Piper?"

28

Home was now a different place to be.

The suburbs seemed endless in obese repetition. The city felt bigger, brighter and ominous. He'd come home to a place he'd never been before.

Only Shwetty knew he was back. The studio had been rented, so he put Buck up at his own place, bringing in beer and supplies as needed. Buck left the Mustang at Everett's, and had been stealthy enough not to have made any contact.

Scared to read the paper, watch the news, or talk to anyone affiliated with the story, Buck was terrified to hear about Madison, his condition. What exactly had happened? Any second he was sure his world might explode into a chaos he couldn't anticipate.

Shwetty saw the change on Buck, the weight, and he wondered when the kid would sing again. Used to be incessant, the singing, and now not a note. He could stay as long as he wanted, no question, but it was important to Shwetty to hear it, to know that the sound was still alive.

Buck hadn't touched his voice. It was the first time in life he'd really let it go. He hadn't even hummed, not since the day he'd met Earl Flood.

To sing was to make the very sound his memory wanted gone. Even to listen, to think about music, it took a kind of courage Buck found himself lacking. In his centermost core, he did know it was what he needed to heal, a knowledge he'd opted to bury in neglect.

What about now? Today and tomorrow? What was there to say?

Doing nothing meant a lot to him. Only in flashes did he attempt to face the questions that were constantly at his back. Most times he could neglect their demands for response, a resolve not to deal with anything, birthing a great ability to ignore.

When Painted Nails played the bowling alley in Renton, and he helped Shwetty load in and out, drinking beer in the back, that was a lot of social activity for Buck, too much. Even that small slice of society gave him a double glance at what he had become. Everyone was impressed to meet him, even the people that'd met him before.

A strange kind of celebrity had been obtained by Buck, a consequence of Piper's notoriety, the television, the tragic and mysterious shadow cast over story of The Wild. The looks from people were more intense, his separation from someone average sharper than before. He drank for free.

It was on the playground, where he finally found himself. Watching from the far side of the area, he could see there were a lot of new faces tearing around, but he spotted some of his kids bouncing about by the fence. Buck had no intention of talking to them.

They were in the past, better left there. He could, maybe way later, finish his education degree, he did love kids, there was a fall-back future, something he could do. That left the big question, the one he'd been avoiding.

What now, Buck? What do you want to do? Just as he found the strength to ask himself the question, to hear it in his head, he was startled by a small voice beside him.

"Buck?"

It was little Anthony, half a head taller than before, standing next to Buck and bewildered by his presence. "Hey, Anthony, how are you?"

The question was met with another.

"Are you coming back?"

"I told you, kid, no one ever gets to go back." The small voice remembered the rest.

"It's all forward from here, huh?"

"That's right, Anthony. What are you doing on this side of the fence?"

Anthony answered with a laugh and rushed Buck with a hug.

Scooping the kid up in a squeeze, Buck deposited him back on the proper side of the fence. Anthony beamed an unstoppable smile and bolted back into the playground. It was after Buck had watched the boy run away and turned to leave that he heard it.

The chords carved into his soul, inflated his spirit, that soft progression, like a lullaby. The music came from a small group of kids, the old-timers, led by Anthony, that had been there with Buck, and their song demanded his ear. Their sound was so real, so honest, that Buck found his lips forming the words.

"Smile child, prayer for the wild . . ."

With a wave to his young friends, Buck left the tune as a soft whisper and made his way in silence back to Shwetty's. After a few pulls off the pipe and a better part of a half-rack Buck found some sleep. Buck seldom dreamed so vividly as he did then.

There he was onstage. With ease he reached down
and picked the crowd up, this wild crowd, his melodic song.
Suddenly there was this place.

Surrounded by trees, way away, like out at the property,
and Piper was there, the cutting sound of her ax, so distinct.
They played together again, like they had so many times before.
That created that same magic, the words and music.

When he woke up he knew. Something had thrown
the switch, he wasn't wasting time anymore, it goes by like
hurricanes, faster things. It was time to get down to the heart
of the matter.

At the end of a gravel road in Burien, rock pounded from
an open suburban garage, a driving rhythm. As Buck sauntered
up the driveway the music stopped. Suddenly Bones bounded
out of the garage and ran up to Buck, almost knocking him
over in embrace.

"Buck? What's up, man? When did you get back? What
the hell?"

"For a bit, I been back for a bit."

"How'd you find me?" "Your mother says hi." "Right."

The two locked eyes, and then said everything else with a
laugh that led them into the garage.

"Hey, this is Stinky here, and Kenny there playing
drums. Guys, this is my friend Buck."

A beer came flying at him, fished from an iced bucket at
Kenny's feet.

"You don't need to tell us who that is, Bones."

Stinky started to noodle on his guitar, Kenny followed
suit, carrying a crisp beat on the drums. Buck cracked his beer
and Bones walked back to his bass, plugged in and slapped
out a quick walk. To be heard, Bones asked his question into
his mike.

"Where are you at with it all, Buck?"

Discarding his shirt, Buck crossed to Bones and removed the mike from the stand.

"Right where I need to be, Bones . . . I'm home."

Turning to Kenny and Stinky, he let out a vocal. It hit just as Bones's bass kicked in, and soared out of their rhythm like a rocket. Buck's voice was fluid, his sound filled with a smile.

29

It was a million miles after midnight and Buck was as cool as a body could be.

He threw himself into music and playing and partying. His life became a nonstop turnstile of friends and activities. He was letting every day peel away, watching a slow firewall of time build between him and his past.

Jamming almost every night with Bones and the boys, they were just finding the sound of their new band. He'd kept Shwetty up until morning every other night. They'd play past dawn, then eat hashbrowns and have Bloody Mary's with the sunrise.

Leaving the club in a gaggle, a whole pack of drunken ear-blasted louts staggered down the street, singing behind Buck as he led another round, a young laughing lady under each arm.

Waking up in a condo down by the waterfront, Buck left the couch he'd crashed on. Finding his shoes, he hazily put the pieces of the night together, stepping over several sleeping bodies, and let himself out. Early enough to be still kind of drunk, he decided the clouds would soon split and it was going to be a nice day. So he opted for a casual walk rather than the bus down to Shewtty's place.

Grub some cereal, stretch out and sleep all day, that was his plan as he walked up the steep stairs. He made it to the cereal and ate the rest of Shwetty's pizza. The last thing he did was collect his messages on the way to bed.

Robert had called twice, about the tribute album for Piper, and a big show, maybe a tour. Everywhere Buck went there was another message from Robert. Seemed he was near hysterical to talk to him.

Would he play the show? Was he interested in the album? What exactly was he up to?

Robert's messages weren't what sobered Buck up. It was one from Jacklyn Wright's assistant. There'd been a break in the case and he was to call in immediately.

Belting down some coffee and with the phone in his hand, he sat down to think. A break in the case. What did that mean, exactly?

Every possibility scared him and it was well after office hours when he finally dialed the number and asked to speak to Jacklyn. Her office plugged him into her cell-phone and she answered briskly. She was in the middle of a location shoot near the beach and had no time for pleasantries.

Apparently a man named Madison Webb had been hospitalized after a brutal robbery at his home in Eastern Washington. It was on a routine search of his home that local authorities found graphic photographs and assorted paraphernalia they referred to as a rape kit, and when they started to really look around, personal items and identifications of near a dozen missing young ladies were found, including Piper. Madison was being held in custody at the hospital, recently upgraded from critical to stable condition.

The news opened up all the wounds Buck had been burying with bottles and beer. Everything he felt for his sister was still alive, and now the piercing fear of what would happen with Madison addled him, almost as much as he still thought about August.

She was actually with him all the time, just not in person, the sound of her voice. Replaying everything she said to him, every moment they spent together, Buck was pissed the only picture he had of her was in his mind. He ached for the sight of her, for her touch.

Calling the diner several times, he talked to the cook and nobody had heard any word. He did everything he could think of, even put a personal in the local rag, and found himself walking to the market not to stand on his brick, but to see if she might be there. It seemed August was going to have to find him, if she wanted to.

Everett probably got the call as well and Buck figured it was time to deal with that. He wanted to tell Everett what happened, maybe prepare him for what might yet come, but he thought better. With Madison alive, and in a hospital or not, there would be no telling what Everett might do now.

Buzz had opened a jazz club in Tacoma and was running the show. Buck sat at the end of the bar and watched as the big man worked the lunch crowd. When he turned to see Buck he let out a shout and came from around the bar.

Over a couple beers in the balcony Buck unloaded his story, the first and only time he gave words to the entire tale. Buzz sat listening in silence after Buck was done speaking, he quietly sipped from the beer sitting before him, nodding his head ever so slightly. His face stayed solid and motionless, one might think he hadn't heard, but the tear rolling on his cheek gave him away.

After another few beers, Buzz gave Buck a ride to FW and dropped him off at the convenience store by Everett's house. After setting Buck up with a fat bag of grass and the solid advice to go see his father, Buzz made a direct point; if there was ever anything, or anybody, that needed doing, they

were done as fast as Buck could ask, no questions. He made
Buck promise to come back down to the club before too long,
then shot him a knowing wink and drove off.

It was early evening and as Buck bought himself some
nachos, Everett was hitting a new all time low just a couple
blocks away. The exact straw that broke his proverbial back
was that call from Jacklyn Wright's assistant, it had busted him
flat, he fell on black days, ripping into a tailspin without food,
sleep, or sanity for way, way, too long. Nothing made any sense
at all, everything hurt, he was tired of being nauseous, of being
sick, of watching himself waste away to a weakling.

Swallowing from a bottle until it was empty, a full grin
flushed his face. Slowly he staggered to the kitchen sink and
buried his head in the faucet. Staring at the empty bottle, he
gave it a goodbye kiss before dropping it to the floor.

Walking to the kitchen closet, he produced his shotgun
and quickly grabbed the wall to steady himself, pushing off in
the direction of the front room, staggering to his knees. He
ripped the collar of his shirt away from his neck and placed the
shotgun stock on the ground. Pointing the barrel to his head
he slowly embraced the edge of the gun with his cheek.

His face then snapped to a numbed, resigned mask. The
point of the barrel was squarely at his forehead, and there was
an audible click as he pulled the hammer back. Everett closed
his eyes.

In the slight hesitation he took to consolidate his
decision, to resign himself, the shadow and sound of a moving
figure grabbed his attention. He looked up to see Piper
standing above him, she was slowly shaking her head. An
etched expression betrayed his stoned astonishment.

Grabbing a bottle of booze from the kitchen counter,
she held it up to the light and cracked the top, tossing the lid
casually. She began to pour the contents on the floor in front
of her, walking and pouring. In the blink of an eye, she was on

the other side of the room, and then the other, Everett turned, twisting to keep up with her.

"What the . . . ?"

Again she was on the other side of the room, now with a bottle in each hand, splashing firewater all about. Flooding the floors and soaking the walls, liquor continued to flow from the bottles far past the point of reason. Then, in a sweeping and extreme gesture of finality, Piper furiously let the bottles fly.

They smashed against the wall beside Everett. In a reel of reaction, he jostled the shotgun against the wall and blasted into the stove, creating a shower of sparks. In a flash the flame sprang from the floor and licked at the walls, beginning to devour the house.

A ring of fire quickly blazed about, and Everett was abruptly left in the middle. Piper was instantly an inch from his face. She softly voiced the message with a single word.

"Forgive."

With a kiss to his cheek, she began dowsing him with the bottle, drowning him in booze. As it cascaded over his head he reacted with a violent shake. Up to his feet, he clenched the shotgun in his hands.

Soaked and shivering, Everett became frantic. He moved in a stumble toward her, but she was gone, and then there, and over there, and gone again. Everywhere he looked, he just missed her, a flash, a flicker of her image, and then only the fire raged around him.

Holding the gun up for protection, he shouted to every sighting, to every sound. Still glimpsing the image of his daughter in smoke and flames, Everett became tangled in a visual and visceral confusion. It was too much, this is past where he'd given up, more than he was ever ready for, and what began with the frustrated cry of a child quickly grew to a raw howl.

Buck had smelled smoke down by the convenience store. It wasn't until he passed the first tight grouping of pressboard homes that he saw the thick black, saw about from where it was coming. The wildest of thoughts ran through his mind, and he hit a full sprint in a second.

Rushing down the driveway, he could hear his father's hysterics coming from inside the house, and he ran into the stoking inferno without a thought. Ten feet inside the door he was as taken aback by the visual state and manic presence of Everett as the flames bounding about. Instantly he became wary of the shotgun, aware of the danger, yet pressed to hurry by the singeing assault of the growing fire, he wasted no time.

"Everett, give me that gun." "Just here. Piper . . ."

"We have to leave. Now." "Piper was here."

Everett's flat-footed defense weakened when his attention was caught by a flame attempting to ignite his torn shirt, he turned to slap at it, moving the shotgun about frantically. Buck took his opening and snatched at the barrel, but Everett pulled back quickly. The gun was suddenly pointing directly at Buck, who responded steadily with a firm and parental tone.

"Enough, Everett, enough." "What?"

Everett reacted with a jerk as Buck continued to move toward him, hoisting the gun from his hip to his shoulder, attempting to sharpen his aim, slurring his words.

"Get back . . ."

"Is this what it is, Everett? Is this it?"

Steadily getting closer, Buck reached his arms open wide, an invitation.

"Then go ahead, take that best shot . . ."

An easy arm's length from Everett, the muzzle pointed at Buck's head, his breath touched the barrel. ". . . anytime."

Everett answered with a gritted jaw and tears tore down his cheeks, his breaking voice cracked a last resistive cry.

"She was . . . Piper."

Everett had retreated as far as the fire would allow. Quickly he began to waver, exhausted and collapsing, from the heat, stress, and emotion around his pathetic line of defense, his shotgun. Buck's voice carried the tone of a quiet confession, a candid truth.

"Was."

The statement sapped the last essence of Everett.

Everything became heavy, his breathing a thick labor. The weight of the shotgun in his arms was hopeless, his eyes impossible to keep open, and he finally let go.

As Everett collapsed, Buck knocked the shotgun from his hands and slung him over his back. Struggling with the weight in a stagger, Buck emerged from the house as it engulfed in flame, escaping as the thundering sound of collapse crashed behind them.

The scream of sirens greeted Buck as he made his way across the yard, his face awash in flashing colored light. There was the first fire truck pulling to a stop in the driveway. That was his finish line.

30

"After a month of intensive hospital care, Madison Webb was set to be indicted this morning."

Jacklyn's speech was the narration to snapshot images of seven young ladies, Piper being the second to last shown.

"But last night, Webb found another way out. He wrestled a handgun from an attending officer, then took his own life."

The visual sequence ended with a black and white photograph of Madison.

"Watch our two-hour special this weekend, 'Madison Webb: The Mind and Life of a Killer.'"

Shifting her position for the close-up, she was diligent as ever.

"This is Jacklyn Wright . . . Welcome Home."

It'd been a long time since Everett had been coherent enough to coordinate doing anything at a prearranged time, even something as simple as catching the special report about Piper, knowing when it was airing and following through by watching it. The segment held no information he hadn't already been filled in on by Jacklyn's assistant prior to broadcast. But it was all too vivid to watch the television

241

recount the facts, and despite the quick answer and tidy ending provided by the show, Everett still had a lot of questions.

Where was Piper, her body? What exactly had happened, exactly? Just what was this thing all the people at the hospital called closure?

There was nothing that would be closed, ever. There were no quick answers that would ever let him or anyone else off the hook. He knew there would never be a day that his thousands of questions about the specific instances and actions that led to this tragedy wouldn't haunt him.

As he was released from the hospital, hopping a cab towards home, Everett knew everything that had happened rendered a reality that anyone involved would have to live with from here on out, for the remainder of their lives. From where he was now, it seemed like that might be a very great distance, or perhaps a very short one. After weeks of shaking in that sick-bed he was so sober as to be scared, finally discerning the depraved distance he'd gone, and wondering where he'd go now.

He knew it had been leveled, that it was a total loss, but the charred pile of burnt wreckage, the sight of his house, shocked him. Slivers of his memory recalled vividly the fire, the flame and confusion. When Everett actually saw the remains, the ruins, he felt feeble, diminished.

The small house was gone, but the detached garage had no idea anything had ever happed. It stood still and unaffected like a sublime monument, some statue. Everett took a moment to look at the garage, to stare it down, and then walked to what had been the side door of his house.

A fresh bandage on his face and the aching quality of his movement were a constant reminder of how recent the fire was. Walking into the middle of the charred ruin, his eyes searched the remains of what had been his home. His eyes fixed on the blackened form of a vodka bottle resting at his feet; kicking at it in inspection he was thrown into memory.

Looking to the driveway he saw himself as a younger man, driving a convertible and wearing a cowboy hat, his beautiful young wife Grace in the passenger seat. Watching the couple park and get out of the car, he saw Piper as a child emerge from the backseat. She grabbed the hand of her mother and the two exited the car.

Wincing as he witnessed himself drinking from a bottle, he shirked away only to find another vision of his same young self now sitting on the couch in the front room. He was badly injured and wrapped in gauze from the car accident, the incident that had changed his life. A woman in a nurse's outfit handed him his toddler son, his little girl Piper sitting beside.

Gripped by his recollection, all around him memories, he saw Piper and Buck being raised, a young man from his little boy, his girl becoming a rebellious adolescent, then a young woman. He revisited it all in glimpses, in instants, so much burnt into his mind, a school bus, the splash and laugh of summer, the heat of his temper, the depth of their love. The first time he'd heard Buck singing down by the lake and knew, the moment he gave his guitar to Piper, he remembered it all.

The familiar sound of strings retrieved Everett to a presence of mind. Hearing the guitar play before had been eerie, unsettling to the point of madness, but now it sounded like the old friend it was. Walking into the driveway, he squared off with the detached garage and its recurring melody.

Approaching with a steady stride, Everett unlocked the door and it opened with a low squeal. He switched on the dirty overheads and stepped into the room. Buck had crashed here some of the last week and a lot of the gear was stacked and stored like before.

To Everett it was more than a reminder. It was a scary preservation of so much that had been. Amongst the piles of gear and nostalgia, illuminated by a direct shaft of dim light, the guitar sat center on its stand.

A slight shiver ran across Everett and he breathed back a wave of emotion. It was right then, with a mind as clear as it ever was going to get, he knew what to do. With a determined grimace and a gradual nod that said he understood, he was ready to surrender to the challenge.

Here it is.

Everett grabbed a stool and walked up to the guitar.

Putting the stool down with a firm placement, a rigid determination, he removed his jacket and tossed it on the couch. Sitting down on the stool, Everett studied the guitar.

With a brave face he reached out and strummed the strings as it sat in its stand. The open chord filled the room. It was the sound, that voice, his first love.

After a pause that could've been forever, he picked up the guitar. His hands moved on instinct, strumming and dialing, it tuned quite quickly, and then he held the neck still. A slow tap of his boot beat out a steady rhythm and with its crisp percussion, Everett began to play.

With the fluid ease of a professional his fingers greeted the guitar. His body was filled with a feeling so long forgotten that it was overwhelming, so physical and so real, it demanded every bit of his attention. Fiddling with riffs and remembering melodies he'd lost to time, Everett became so absorbed that the hours flew far away.

Finally finding the opening to 'Touch of Grace,' he was amazed how easy it was for him to play, how nimble his hands were, how little his feel had diminished. It was everything Everett used to be, and despite himself, it was what had endured, the music. It'd been way too long since he'd felt like this, like him.

"You are good."

Leaning against the doorway, Buck was listening, the first time he heard his father play.

"Maybe was."

Buck walked over and stood next to Everett, who remained seated and lifted the guitar, presenting it to Buck.

"I think your sister would've wanted you to have this." Raising his hands, Buck stepped back away from the guitar, his head slowly shaking off the present. "I'm a singer."

It was soft and specific, what he had to say. "That's your guitar, so play."

There was a beat of suspense. Buck met his father's eyes with a solid resolve. Finally Everett broke into a slight laugh and he shook his head.

"Well, I guess you finally showed me what it is, didn't you, Buck?"

Lowering the guitar back to his lap, Everett let the beginning of 'Touch of Grace' fly from his fingers. Sitting on the arm of the couch, Buck caught the rhythm on his knee and began to sing. In the music they were all there together, the entire Wild family, right then, and forever.

31

Robert rubbed clear the lenses of his glasses, then surveyed the old and elaborately decorated auditorium with a squint.

Including the balcony, the space sat around eight to ten thousand. At one time it'd been restored to new, but was now showing the wear of a constantly used venue. Walking from the backstage into the house his passage was dimly lit by the green exit sign hovering over the double doors.

"Hello . . . hello?"

Venturing further onto the partially-lit stage, he was standing in the middle of the proscenium when he called out again.

"Hello? Buck?"

The slapping sound of clapping hands revealed Buck. Slouched in a seat near the back center of the house, Buck's sneakers were up on the chair ahead of him. Slowly he rose to his feet, and eased to the stage edge, with a kind tease.

"That's a hell of an entrance, you're a natural."

Shielding his eyes with his hand, Robert pivoted to look across the orchestra pit.

"Buck?"

"You've been very busy, haven't you, Robert?" "I live on the phone."

Struggling down from the stage, he handed Buck a small stack of paperwork.

"That's a sweet deal, kid, a real rock and roll swindle." "Swindle?"

"A huge cash advance, Buck, really."

The magnum pull from his smoke underlined the severity of Robert's statement and he continued.

"Everyone plays an instrument wants in, this could go up for album of the year, all three of your songs made the cut, and the producer flipped over that one with the kids singing those backups."

Robert's phone rang, he glanced then clicked it off, looking to Buck with stone sincerity.

"They want you in the studio yesterday, to help finish the mix on the children samples."

When Buck finally contacted Robert and agreed to the first meeting, his world spun into a change, something so new. The tribute album would be widely released with a surge of promotion and the bulk of proceeds going to charity. Robert was on a roll, all of Piper's work was being re-released, and he'd even found a record deal for a pet local band of his.

Buck's original takes with Piper were already mixed into the song, so he didn't put down much more than some backup. Recording the children was the big challenge. Contacting the parents of his favorite kids, a few that had left already, and corralling them to the studio, then commanding their attention long enough to get it down, proved to be an exhausting afternoon, but it sounded way better than even he thought it would.

"Finish mixing those tracks, and after the gig on Friday, you're a free agent."

Robert handed a pen to Buck, who scanned the documents, initialed, and signed on several lines. Since he'd hooked up with Robert, there had been more paperwork and breakdowns and arrangements than Buck could keep up with. He'd begun to realize that wherever one starts, whatever they do, of business are something that have to be learned.

"You understand this is going to get attention? Buck, put a polka band together right now an you will get signed, maybe even sell, you get it?"

What Robert said was true. All this was a lot bigger deal than Buck expected. There was far more time, effort, and money involved than he dreamt.

Maybe when your dreams begin to come true that's the way things are. He knew what brought him this far this quick, that he was standing on Piper's shoulders, but also that he'd paid in spades for any advantage, and when the show started, he'd own every note. He went to bed and woke up a couple more times, and then it was the day he'd been waiting for.

There were two warm-up bands, and after a brief break the crowd grew rabid with an anticipated pounding that shook the house. Three guys, from two of the biggest bands around, took the stage and the audience roared at the sight of the rock stars. The musicians all knew Piper well, each wrote for the album in the true sense of a tribute, out of reverence, memory, and love.

Buck only knew the bass player, he was a brilliant guy with a vibrant energy that reminded him of Sklyer. They'd become friends and he'd made Buck feel like one of the boys during rehearsals. It was his bass that cued the house to dissolve slowly into a sharp red hue.

As the music began to grow behind him, the brightest of lights found Buck centerstage. He thrust his arms open in wide greeting to the audience. A wild smile leapt from his face and ignited the auditorium.

The screaming applause of the audience voiced their manic approval, their anticipation. Buck started with a growl that elevated to a low mournful hum, sounding more like an instrument than a voice. With a presence smooth and magnetic, his sound like a weapon, he captured the cheering, whistling, crowd turning them to stone silence in seconds.

Singing two of his three songs without a flaw, he exited and watched the show from backstage until the last number, until it was his turn again. A series of artists took the spotlight, there were several tunes Buck really liked, but everything smoked. It fired him up to be in their company, and finally it was up to Buck to bat clean-up.

The guitarist played the lithe preamble to 'Smile Child,' and the pre-recorded sound of a playground, the laughs, cheers, and squeals of children broke over the house. It increased in volume with the light, until the rhythm kicked in with its heavy change. Right on time, Buck's voice split the air and rode into the music.

He moved to the edge of the stage, singing the first verse, and during the chorus the children filled the song with a choral, almost gospel feel. The crowd erupted with a large blast of cheering and applause. By the third time the chorus came around, the audience lit the house with their lighters and sang it over, and again, as an anthem, in unison with the children.

"Smile child, prayer for the wild, sing me a song, let the smile shine a while . . ."

Cooling to a watery blue, the stage lights dimmed and the spot singled on Buck. Reaching his right arm up, he stretched a fist way above his head. He belted out the last note so far that the heavens were forced to hear him, to look and take note, to recognize a true moment of triumph and grace.

A huge buzz of humanity swarmed Buck backstage. There wasn't anyone who didn't want to touch and talk to him. So many questions and so much attention, it tainted the energy he'd gained from the show, and brought on a blunt feeling of isolation.

Dodging Robert and a pack of suits he saw pursuing him, Buck ducked into the freight elevator. Up on the roof he went to the edge, where he stood and looked down at the milling of cars and leaving people. He sat there with an undeniable float of satisfaction, of accomplishment, letting time pass until he was fairly sure he could escape without a fuss. a bunch of people still about, but Buck was able to hide in a slouch and pass right by. Exiting out the backstage door, a light sprinkle started to fall and he began down the brick alley, figuring to take the bus back to Shwetty's.

Leaning against the wall, just across the way, she was all smiles. His spirit lifted at the sight and he sprinted with a loud shout. It wasn't until he touched her, until he took her lips and she held him closely, tight to her breathing body, that he let himself believe she was real, that they'd made it right here, right now, that it was August.